IF YOU CHERISH ME

CIARA KNIGHT

If You Cherish Me
Book III
Sugar Maple Series
Copyright ©2020 by Ciara Knight
All rights reserved.

****To receive a FREE starter library (Two free books) AND an alert of Ciara's next book releases, go to Ciara's Exclusive Reader group click here. ****

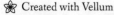 Created with Vellum

READER LETTER

Dear Reader,

I've love all the reader emails and comments about the Sugar Maple series! I'm so excited that you've been enjoying this small town, because I know I've really enjoyed writing these books. This story specifically was a joy to write. Sometimes characters just talk to me and it makes everything click. Don't get me wrong, there was a ton of editing still involved. Of course, with a dyslexic writer there is always a lot of editing!

Since I've enjoyed this series so much, and many of you have sent questions about Davey, I've decided to write a Christmas story set in the 1940s about Davey as a child. This will still be a sweet romance, but I'm going to give you an inside look at why Davey is the way he is.

In the meantime, I hope you enjoy If You Cherish Me, a sweet story about a man struggling with his past and a girl wanting a brighter future with the occasional Davey cameo and a new/old love interest in his life.

Sincerely,
Ciara

ONE

The midmorning sun blasted the spring flowers with summer heat. Since when did the Tennessee mountains reach blistering hot temperatures in April? Felicia pushed as many potted plants and flowers into the shade of the large maple tree as she could manage.

Jackie sauntered up in a flowing summer dress that swished with each perfect-postured step. The contrast of the pale green made her dark, red hair even more vibrant. "So much for the Fabulous Five sticking together."

Felicia patted her gloves together to rid them of some of the excess dirt onto the grass to her side and then blinked up at her. "What are you talking about? Did I miss a get-together or something?"

"Ha, so much for the negotiator. You didn't even try to put my name in the hat for the Spring Festival or to be next on Knox's show." The way Jackie lifted her long thin nose into the air and placed her perfectly manicured hands on her hips told Felicia she was in trouble. And Jackie had a point. Everyone knew that Jackie longed to star in the Knox Brevard internet show but had been passed over twice already.

"I didn't have a say in his show. I'm just following what I was told to do by Ms. Horton." Felicia was being honest but not forthcoming. If she wanted to truly share why she hadn't thought about Jackie joining the Spring Festival, she'd have to confess that her business was thriving so much she didn't have time to breathe, let alone think about a friend. That would only lead to hurting Jackie's feelings due to her failing dress shop, which was, of course, the reason she needed her business highlighted on the Knox Brevard show. "As for the festival, what do you mean?" Felicia stood, removed her gloves, and slid them into her apron pocket that Mary-Beth had hand embroidered with *The Tranquil Maple* on the front along with two bright pink flowers.

"I mean," Jackie said, slow and drawn-out as if to make her point more obvious so Felicia could follow, "Carissa is selling baked goods and passing out free tastings, Mary-Beth is doing the same but with coffee, and you're doing flowers and plants. Even Stella organized a classic car show. Where do I fit into all this? I'm not sure why I've stayed in Sugar Maple so long if I'm not wanted."

"Don't say that. We want you here." Felicia saw the telltale sign of jealousy with Jackie's twitching cheek. What could she say to smooth things over, though? She had a point. They'd all been so busy. Felicia hadn't even had time for her own grandmother, who needed her most. She was desperate for help at her nursery, more help than her assistant who never, well, assisted. She scanned the parking spaces that circled the town square, but there was still no sign of Lacey.

"Are you even listening to me?" Jackie tapped her size-six heeled sandals that were sparkly gold with tiny beads on the straps. The girl knew her fashion.

"Yes." Felicia stood, untied her apron, rolled it, and then tucked it next to her gardening bag that Mary-Beth had made to match the apron. "Why didn't you organize a fashion show?"

"For this town? Why would anyone care about that?" Jackie crossed her arms and eyed the town square down the end of that nose that always pointed in the directions she wanted to go.

Felicia closed her eyes for a second, digging for possibilities to make Jackie feel more a part of the town. She needed the five to stay together. No, not just her—the entire town needed the Fabulous Five to stay together. As Ms. Horton always said, the Fabulous Five kept people united through events, blessings, and hugs. Not to mention the occasional intervention when a town resident needed some extra help, like when they'd worked on Jake's garden a few months ago after his mother died. "Charity? Those always sell out. You could've done that. Hey, it's not too late. The festival runs all week."

Jackie looked at Felicia as if she'd grown a rose bush out of her temple. "Seriously? Me, charity? What charity would I even work with?"

Felicia shrugged. "Don't know. Something you care about. Something the entire town would care about." She tried not to ask if Jackie cared about anything or anyone else besides herself; that would only fuel the discontent. Besides, deep down, Jackie was a wounded soul who lashed out to protect herself. She wasn't a bad person. She had a heart. It just needed to be dug up from wherever she'd buried it while she was away for a decade living in the big city. "I heard the kids at the day care needed—"

"Kids? You don't know me at all. I'm the only one of this friend group who never wants those sniveling little creatures to make stains on my skirt and leave snot on my collar."

Felicia scanned the area once more, willing Lacey to show with the company truck full of the rest of the plants. The senior bus stuttered and tooted black smoke out of the tail pipe at the turn onto the square. It jerked and coughed and belched to a front parking space. "Guess we better call Stella." Felicia brushed her palms together to rid them of any soil residue before she reached for her phone.

Jackie slid her purse off one elbow and onto the other. "I don't know why everyone thinks Stella's so gifted. She can't even fix a van the elders use."

"She tries, but the van is only put together by duct tape and prayer according to Stella. She said she doesn't know how much longer she can patch it." Felicia abandoned her plants, texted Stella, and went to help the elders off the bus. "Good morning, Davey. You coming to help with some decorating?"

"Sure thing, missy. I'm ready to make my big cameo appearance on the Knox Brevard show. He said we're needed as extras for your segment." Davey did a jig. He looked like a scarecrow that had elbows like the tin man before he was oiled.

"Sounds perfect. I'm hoping my flowers get here soon, though." Felicia eyed the four corners of the square. Still no sign of her truck or Lacey.

"That cousin of yours not doing her job again? She's probably up to no good. I don't know why you put up with her."

"She's family and she tries. She's just a little scattered at times since she got a boyfriend in her life." Felicia neglected to mention she didn't like the boy Lacey had chosen. No need to get Davey riled up.

"You know you can't save everyone, right?" Davey winked, his eye disappearing between wrinkles. "You've got enough strays on your property to start a zoo."

Felicia helped Ms. Melba off the bus and passed her to Davey. "I'm not trying to save anyone."

"Really? What about that man, Declan? I hear you took him food and such."

Felicia felt heat rise to her cheeks, even though she was standing in the shade. "I was just being neighborly."

"Neighbors are people who have homes. Campers don't count. They aren't permanent." Davey swished his lips, making little bubbles that caused him to look rabid.

Jackie flipped her hair over her shoulder and shook her head. "She's obsessed with strangers. It's friends she can't remember."

Ouch. "Don't pull any punches." Felicia faced Jackie, ready to share the entire truth about why she'd been so busy.

Jackie must've sensed it too because she waved her hands dismissively and said, "Stella still hasn't fixed that bus, huh?"

"No. Guess you'll have to take us all back to the center after this. I've always wanted to ride in that little sporty car of yours." Davey wiggled his eyebrows, making them look like battling silver caterpillars.

Jackie chuckled and offered Davey her arm. The girl always liked the men, no matter what age. Poor Ms. Melba looked dejected.

Felicia offered her arm and escorted her to the bench. "Tell you what... I have a special centerpiece I need finished. Do you think you could help with that?"

Ms. Melba lit up like a Golden Lily. "Sure! I'll work real hard for you, hon. Just get me the stuff."

Felicia glanced at the four corners again. Still no sign of Lacey. "I'll get it to you soon. I'm waiting on a delivery. I'll be right back."

Felicia caught up to Jackie and Davey at the other side of the gazebo area. "Can you do me a favor? Can you see if you can find Lacey and my truck? I need to get those flowers from the nursery here before they can start filming, and Knox's crew is due to arrive any minute."

"No need. I know where she's at." Jackie fluffed her hair around her face and sat down by Davey's side.

"Great. Where?" Felicia asked, hopeful she was close.

"She's in Riverdale with her new boyfriend. Apparently she wanted your truck so she could go visit him and never had any intention of helping you today."

Felicia wilted. "No. She wouldn't."

"She would and she did." Jackie gave her the I-told-you-to-fire-her look.

Felicia lowered to the bench on the other side of Davey, wanting to admonish Jackie for not giving her this information sooner, but timing for dramatic affect was her specialty. "I can't believe this."

"I can. I told you she needed to be run out of town. Just like that Declan guy. Look at him over there, still begging for a job. I should go tell him we don't need his kind here in Sugar Maple. We're good people and don't have no room for no ex-cons." Davey spit when he spoke like a venomous snake ready to strike.

Felicia shot him a sideways glower. "Now, Davey, there's no reason to be ugly. That man stood up to Stella's father to help her and ended up with a massive bruise on his shoulder. He's lucky nothing was broken."

"Not a good deed if you brought the man into town in the first place," Davey huffed.

Felicia watched Declan pop in and out of several stores with a smile on the way in and slumped shoulders on the way out. "Did you put out a no-hire mandate on him?"

Davey scrunched his lips and smacked them. "Maybe."

Felicia shook her head and sighed. "Not nice. I expect better from you." She stood, intending to go talk to the object of Davey's scorn. When Declan Mills first came to Sugar Maple with Stella's father, Jackie had indeed been right when she called him a convict. He hadn't tried to make excuses for what happened, but she had heard him mumble under his breath something about his mother and protecting her from Stella's father. At least, that's what she'd thought she'd heard him say.

There had to be some truth to it, because the man had been nothing but polite, kind, and well-mannered, and not once had he been less than a gentleman around her, so she was willing to give him the benefit of the doubt and an opportunity to prove Davey and the rest of the town wrong. The poor guy had no idea the prejudice he'd be facing, but Felicia did. She'd been looked down on for so long from certain members of the community due to her mixed race that she'd felt the full sting of judgment over the years.

"Going to pick up another stray?" Jackie asked.

Felicia watched Declan, a healthy-looking, muscular man with well-kempt hair and attitude stand at the corner waiting for some piece of good news, and she had one for him. "No, I'm finally taking your advice, Jackie."

"It's about time. Which one?"

"I'm going to demote my assistant and hire a new one."

"You mean fire." Jackie bolted up from the bench and uncharacteristically hotfooted it in front of Felicia. "Wait, you're not thinking—"

"That I'm going to hire Declan as my new assistant? Yes. Accuse me of picking up another stray. I don't care. Everyone deserves a second chance. And apparently I'm the only one in town willing to give him one. So much for small-town welcomes. You both should be ashamed of yourselves."

"He's an ex-con. Not a visitor from out of town," Jackie said, as if Felicia had forgotten.

She brushed past Jackie, knowing she'd never convince anyone else that Declan deserved a chance. Prejudice lived in all towns, no matter how loving and special they were. And it was her job to show Sugar Maple they were wrong. Declan had obviously had a rough start, something Felicia could relate to, and he needed one person in the world to give him an opportunity. She paused at the curb. "Besides, I need the help. It's not like you're going to break a nail or get your hands dirty. Sometimes we need to open our eyes to what opportunities are around us, however unlikely they seem."

Davey pushed up from the bench with a grimace. "You're making a mistake."

Felicia shrugged. "It's my mistake to make." She crossed the road, leaving her loving town family behind to extend a true Sugar Maple welcome to a man who'd been judged and sentenced by the elders without a trial.

TWO

Declan checked off the barber shop, the last potential job opportunity in town. If he didn't find something soon, he'd have to search elsewhere if he wanted to be able to make his restitution payment and not end up back in jail.

He glanced around the quaint town square full of residents setting up for some event. He longed to be a part of the group, but no one liked outsiders in this town. Especially outsiders with a criminal record.

Sugar Maple could be on the front page of *Southern Living* or some other magazine. Especially with all the plants arranged around half of the square that sprouted spring flowers in a spectrum of vibrant colors. It had to be the expert work of the beautiful and kind Felicia Hughes, based on the perfect backdrop of earthy greens with pops of color. She stood at the curb with the friend of hers he'd overheard being called Judas Jackie. He wasn't sure what that was about, but they'd seemed like good friends when he'd seen them together. The man shuffling toward them from a nearby bench to Jackie's side was none other than Davey, who'd threatened to run Declan out of town several times already.

Declan's gaze skimmed over them like dust in the air and settled on the bright light of the mesmerizing Felicia. She had a kind heart and a good nature, too. The type of young woman who was pleasant to be around and pleasant to look at. Of course, just getting out of twenty months of incarceration with no members of the opposite sex in sight probably made her look even more beautiful than normal. That could explain why he'd been captivated by her like no other woman he'd ever met in his life.

If he had the opportunity to describe Felicia to his mother without her screaming at him for five minutes, he'd say she was exotic with hair the color of a moonless night sky that contrasted with her light complexion. Sparkling, crystalized silver-blue eyes distracted him into a mumbling fool each time she'd blessed him with a greeting. A true unique beauty who belonged standing in the middle of her floral arrangements on an advertisement poster.

He took a moment to inhale the sweet smells of the town—baked goods, coffee, and freedom. Each second was precious when there was sun over his head, and anything was better than the smell of Clorox or body odor he'd lived with for so long.

Guessing the event was for residents only, he figured he should make himself scarce before Davey shook his fists at him. He turned right and headed for the four-way stop.

"Wait, I need you." Felicia's sweet voice carried in the spring-perfumed breeze, halting him before he reached the corner. "I need you to do me a huge favor if you would. I'll pay you, of course."

He turned for a close-up view of Felicia with her hair pulled back, accentuating her long neck and pronounced cheekbones. The way she spoke in a rush made his pulse go from disappointed slow bass drum to a tympanic symphony. "It wouldn't be a favor if you paid me. How can I help?"

"It's more of a job than a favor, then. I'll pay you. I need you to take me to the nursery and help transport the rest of the plants here as quick as possible. Knox has a crew headed here now. I'd ask the senior bus driver, but the bus broke down again, and Jackie's car is a little thing. Besides, she'd never allow dirt in her Porsche."

He held up one hand to slow her speech. "I'd be happy to help."

She let out the longest breath and dropped her hands to her sides, slumping a little with extra drama. "Thanks so much. You're a lifesaver."

"It's no big deal. I didn't have anything else going on right now anyway. Come on." He'd been called many things since arriving in Sugar Maple. None of them were so kind. It didn't escape him that she'd said that a little louder than necessary and she'd shot a glance at everyone nearby, as if to make sure they'd heard her. This woman had been so nice, considering she had to know his history. Why would she ever trust a man with a record like his? She had no idea he'd served time for a crime he didn't commit. If his own mother didn't believe the truth, this woman shouldn't.

To his disappointment, she took off at Davey-on-free-cookie-day speed instead of a romantic afternoon stroll. She stood as high as his shoulder, so he was surprised at how fast her small legs moved. Not that she was short, since he was over six-three himself. "What happened with your delivery?"

She blinked up at him over the rim of her sunglasses.

"Sorry. Not my place to ask."

"No, it's not that. It's just that I'm not too happy with my cousin right now. It's nothing to be worried about, though. I'm sure she has a good explanation. It's just poor timing to have her flake on me. I've got so much going on. Not that I can't handle it."

He opened the camper door and hoped she didn't mind the old look of it. Good thing he'd tidied up his suitcase and made his bed this morning before going out to look for a job. "If she's working for you, you shouldn't have to handle it on your own."

"I can't argue with that. And to be honest, I'm going to have to have an uncomfortable conversation with her as soon as she returns from Riverbend." Felicia climbed into the passenger seat, and he jerked the seat belt twice to get it to release.

"Sorry. It's an old but reliable motorhome." He handed it to her and stepped back. "You need to push, then pull, and then shove it in until it clicks."

He shut the door and rounded the camper to settle into the driver's seat, where he found her fumbling with the buckle. "Here, let me."

He covered her hand gently with his, causing his breath to catch. It had been a long time since he'd been this close to a woman, so he had to force his darn fingers to not lace between hers like some sixteen-year-old boy trying to put the moves on his first date.

Click.

He sat away from the light floral smell he assumed came from all the plants she worked with, because no one smelled that good naturally. Forcing his thoughts on the task in front of him instead of the distraction at his side, he revved the engine, which sputtered, clunked, and then rolled into a purr. "Let's go."

"Seriously, you're such a blessing. I don't know what I would've done." She looked over her shoulder. "I hate to put plants in your home... I promise to spread blankets out, and if any soil spills, I'll vacuum it."

"Don't think twice about it. I've been living with a ton of men in a small space for almost two years. I can handle a little soil in my home."

She sat back and stared forward as if his words were a shock to her.

He didn't like the uneasiness left between them. "You knew that I'd served time." He quirked an eyebrow at her, knowing he had to make sure she understood this point so she didn't get any weird ideas about being attracted to him or wanting to go out with him. He didn't trust himself to say no to her, so it was up to her to keep the necessary distance between them.

"I know. It's just, you don't have to remind me every time we run into each other." Felicia pulled her hair clip out, allowing long dark strands to cascade over her shoulders before she twisted her hair into a bun and secured it again. "It's as if...I don't know...you want to keep me at a safe distance from you. Did I do something to offend you?"

"No." He slowed and took the turn toward her nursery carefully so he didn't cause anything to fall free from his camper. "It's me, not you."

"Oh, great. We haven't even been on a date, and I got the it's-me-not-you speech. I've never been rejected before I even made a pass at someone." She winked at him, and he ran off the road.

Dishes clinked, and a bar of soap he'd used this morning at the truck stop slid out of the container and flung against the wall. He corrected his path onto the asphalt and drove straight and true down the two-lane road. "I don't think you have to ever worry about being rejected."

She pointed to a driveway with a sign out front that read *The Tranquil Maple*, so he turned onto the gravel drive and pulled to the fence. Barking dogs, a mule, a pig, and some chickens ran wild on the other side.

"You're far too beautiful and nice to worry about that."

"Then why?" she said in a plain tone, as if she'd asked about the weather.

He turned off the engine and gripped the steering wheel. "Because, Felicia Hughes, I find you way too attractive to trust myself not to ask you out. And you deserve far better than me."

"Why do you say that?" She looked at him with the most honest, eyes-open expression.

"I don't want to say it again. You told me you didn't like me reminding you all the time." He smiled with as much charisma as he could manage, but he was sure he looked more like a mad botanist than achieving a friendly flirt.

Felicia offered a reciprocating smile. A small but heart-pumping kind of grin. "Okay, so you went to prison." She opened her door. "Come on, I need you." She flushed, her cheeks turning a slight shade of pink that was alluring and innocent at the same time. "I mean, I need you to assist me with loading, if you don't mind."

He didn't have to be asked twice to spend more time with her. Before she could open the fence, he was by her side, helping to push the chain link gate on wheels out of the way while she shooed the dogs.

"I'm not saying I want to marry you. I just want to be your friend. If I'm being honest, you aren't too bad-looking yourself."

She spoke with a confidence and honesty that took him a moment to comprehend. Even in his former life as a businessman with many dating choices, he couldn't recall another woman like her. Women who were bold and flirtatious, yes, but it was always a game with them. Felicia had a sincerity about her.

Was she flirting? With him? Knowing the truth? "Thanks," he said in a too-surprised tone. Man, he was out of practice with all this flirtation stuff. For a second, he could imagine that he'd never served time and that the world didn't see him as some sort of monster that would steal their money and lives from them.

He moved the camper to the other side of the fence, and

Felicia closed the gate and then hopped back inside, directing him to an area near a small, muted-yellow home with white molding, porch, and trellis half covered by ivy up one side.

"So, friends okay with you?" She held out her dainty hand.

"Sure. Friends." He shook it, trying to ignore the hot flash up his arm.

She pointed to several plants, indicating what needed to be loaded. He joined her near a door on the side of the house, where one of the plants had the most unique color. A dark and mysterious flower that was so deep purple it was almost black but with depth of various shades. "Can you grab those, please? I'll get the ferns."

He lifted four of them in his arms and headed for the side door of the camper. "What are these?"

"Petunia Deep Midnight. I like to add a splash of dark colors with the bright spring flowers so that they pop even more on camera."

She was good at what she did. Of course, he'd been good at his job once, too. He had loved numbers, but now he needed a new career—or at least a job.

Two dogs wanted to help and kept leaping and barking at him.

"Sorry about all the animals," Felicia offered.

"No worries. I love animals." Declan rounded the camper, opened the side door, placed his plants in the far corner, and then took the ones Felicia held out to him.

"Since we're friends now and you have such a desire to remind me about your time behind bars, is it okay if I ask what you went to jail for?"

The smell of freshly watered soil soothed him, despite his fear of the truth. "Embezzlement."

"That all?" She shrugged.

"*That all?*" It was his turn to blink at her. "I was sentenced to two years for felony embezzlement. You do know what embezzlement is, right?"

She popped her hip out and rested a pot on it. "Seriously? I might grow plants, but that doesn't make me stupid."

"I didn't mean... I—"

"Calm down. I'm joking." Felicia handed him the last plant she held, and he tucked it into the corner between the seat and the kitchen cabinet. "Did you do it?"

He froze. The four words no one had ever asked before today. Maybe that was because he'd confessed before they could ever ask. How did he answer her? If he told her the truth, would she believe him? He couldn't face her and see the doubt in her eyes if he told her no, but if he said yes, he couldn't face her look of disappointment. "I'm not sure I want to answer that right now."

Felecia ran over to retrieve more plants and then handed them to him and he placed them inside. "Why?"

"Because you're the first friend I've had in the outside world. I learned before I went in that it was less about innocence and guilt and more about judgment. I don't want to be judged anymore."

She pressed her lips together in a way that made him fear what she'd say next. "My father used to be accused of stealing from the local grocer. One time the sheriff picked him up for loitering to quiet the man down. I still remember riding in the police car with my father as he looked down with tears in his eyes, but I never understood why he was upset. I knew he didn't do it. He never would've stolen from anyone. I didn't know why until years later, but it turned out that the grocer thought my father looked like someone who had broken into his store years earlier, since they both had dark skin."

"That's terrible." Declan didn't like the thought of this

sweet girl seeing her father harassed, let alone ever stepping inside a precinct as a child.

"It was, but it taught me never to judge a man and to always form my own opinion."

"Okay, then, what's your opinion?" He allowed himself a moment to believe her words, that if he told her the truth, she'd accept him at his word.

"I believe you're trustworthy enough to work for me. If I wanted to believe the worst, you committed a white-collar crime and I don't believe you're a physical danger to me or my family, or you were falsely convicted and you're innocent. Either way, I need the help and you're a good worker. I want you to come work for me."

He needed a job more than anything. This could keep him from having to return to jail by giving him the money to make restitution payments and filling his parole criteria. It was too good to be true. The thought of working side-by-side with this full-of-life person who made him smile inside as well as out... More than anything, he wanted to work for her, to spend time with her. And that was a problem. "I can't work for you."

THREE

The front door squealed open, drawing Felicia to the front yard. Her nana stood in the doorway in her morning robe. Felicia silently chastised herself for not getting her grandmother dressed before her day had begun, but she'd run out of time since Lacey hadn't shown to help get everything ready for transport. "What's wrong, Nana?"

"I woke up and no one was here. Thought something happened to you, dear."

Declan joined her, holding two large containers of ferns.

"You can take a break. I'll be right back, and then we can finish loading the rest of those." She trotted to the front steps, where she said to her grandmother, "You shouldn't be out here in your dressing gown. Let's get you inside. I'll fix you something to eat. Ms. Horton said she'd stop by in a bit, but if you want to go into town, you can hang out with Melba and Davey."

"No. Not feeling up to it today." Nana shuffled inside, stumbling over the lip on the threshold of the front door before grabbing hold of her cane. "You go on though. I'm not hungry. I just wanted to make sure my baby girl was okay."

"I'm fine, Nana." Felicia raced for the kitchen, determined to at least make her some toast and coffee.

"No, you're not. You work too hard. You can't do everything for everyone. Now you scoot on out of here. I'll be fine." She picked up a dish towel and swatted at Felicia.

"Okay, but I'll be back in a couple of hours, and then I'll make us a big lunch." Felicia poured her a cup of coffee and set it on the table before rushing to the door. Guilt plagued her, watching her grandmother left behind alone. The woman had been her closest parental figure and ally her entire life, and now she was abandoning her for work. Not that she had a choice. She had to keep money coming in for the medical bills after her grandmother's stroke last year.

Felicia darted outside to the camper, where she discovered Declan closing the side door. She glanced at the spaces where she'd had the flowers. He'd already finished packing everything inside. "Wow, you're a hard worker. And talk about taking initiative. I can't get Lacey to even return a phone call to a client without asking me for permission. Of course, she's young and lacks life experience."

He opened the passenger door and waited for her to step inside. "Just helping out, being a good neighbor is all."

Before she could argue his point, he shut the door, rounded the camper, and hopped into the driver's seat. "Wow, my home's never smelled so good." He chuckled and eyed the plants behind them.

"I've always loved the scent of flowers, fresh-cut grass, and damp soil after a rain." Felicia managed her seat belt this time while the engine roared to life and they headed down the drive with her sweet dogs jumping around them. The donkey lumbered across the drive, slowing Declan's pace for a few moments.

"Is that why you got into your agricultural pursuits?"

Felicia watched the trees and shrubs budding with new life for the summer. It wouldn't be long until she could ship the expensive decorative grass, ground coverings, landscaping shrubs and trees to Nashville for the big chunk of her annual revenue. With the extra rain and mild temperatures, they'd grown well this year, but this meant even more work she needed to manage over the next few weeks. "It's part of the reason."

"What's the other part?"

She studied the soil staining her short nails and fisted her hands to hide them. Jackie would be mortified if she noticed Felicia's chipped, unkempt look. It was tough to keep nails looking good while working in dirt all day, though. "My nana always worked with me in the garden growing up. Somehow she could always tell when I had a rough day at school, and she'd simply hand me galoshes, a hat, and a hand shovel, and we'd head outside."

"It's her *chocolate chip* method, huh?"

"What?"

"You know, a child comes home to chocolate chip cookies and milk to make their day better. Your nana used plants instead. That's why you love gardening so much. It's your welcome-home place."

She never thought about it that way, but he had a point. "I guess." They reached the end of the drive, so she took care of the fence and made sure the animals were safely inside before returning to the camper.

He turned onto the main road headed to town. The rocking motion made her prepare for plants tumbling around, but not one of them moved.

"Does she still garden with you? Your nana? She's the one we saw on the front porch, right?" He asked as if he were truly interested instead of just making small talk or acting like he cared.

On most of her previous dates, she'd found that men tended to ask about the girl for about five minutes, as if they'd been coached by a mother or sister, and then they'd start talking about their important jobs, how big a house they owned, or other life accomplishments. She understood planting flowers and trees wasn't fascinating to most people. *Not that this was a date.* "Yes, that's her. But no, we don't garden together anymore. Not since her stroke a year ago. She lost a lot of function in one arm, and one foot tends to flop at times. I'm afraid I haven't been able to get her to leave the house since she recovered."

"That's a shame. My mother was the opposite. I couldn't keep her home. She'd get out and find trouble wherever she went. By the time I managed to get released, she'd gone from a little distracted and repeating herself, to wandering the streets and giving her money away to bad people."

"You mean Stella's father, right?" she asked, already knowing the answer based on what happened only months earlier.

"Yes." He rolled to a stop at the four-way and then proceeded to the edge of the town square. "I'm afraid that the only way I could get them apart was to put my mother into a home and take him out of town. He'd agreed to stay away from my mother if I drove him to Sugar Maple. I promise I had no idea what he was planning when I brought him here. I've been wanting to apologize to Stella, but Knox won't let me near her. Not that I'm surprised. I wouldn't let me near her either if I were him."

They reached the town square, and Felicia's breath quickened at the sight of the production crew already setting up. "Why would you say that?"

"Because I wouldn't want you near me if I were lucky enough to be your boyfriend."

She smiled at him, but his gaze was laser focused on the parking spot he pulled into. "I'll get this unloaded."

"Not unless you take the job." She unclipped her seat belt and opened the door to a crowd of people staring at her and Declan in his camper.

"I'll think about it, but I don't think it's a good idea."

She didn't even have time to open the side door to get the plants before three of her friends—Carissa, Jackie, and Mary-Beth—whisked her away.

"What're you doing in a car with him?" Jackie scolded.

Mary-Beth held tight to her arm. "I hate to admit it, but Jackie's right. You can be nice all you want, but you shouldn't endanger yourself."

"He's not like that. I promise. You all have it wrong about Declan. He's a nice guy and a total gentleman. Besides, he wasn't put in jail for some deviant crime that would endanger my life. It was a white-collar crime dealing with money in a corporation."

Carissa moved in front of them, halting them near the camera area. "See, girls, we can relax."

Based on Mary-Beth's fingers allowing circulation back into Felicia's arm and Jackie no longer scowling at her, Felicia assumed that the nonviolent nature of his crime eased their worry.

"I'll relax when that criminal is run out of town," Davey shouted from the bench at their side, where he had apparently remained since she'd left the square to get the plants.

Jackie obviously found the camera crew more interesting, so she bolted to where they were setting up.

"Mary-Beth!" Stella hollered from across the square, where she rubbed her hands with a cloth next to the senior bus.

It was nice having all five of them together, even if it was a crazy time that wouldn't allow Felicia to hang out with them at all.

"Sorry, ladies. I promised to be Stella's assistant since her new boyfriend is so busy with the show," Mary-Beth said with an air of surprise, as if they all didn't already know that Sassy Stella had started dating the internet sensation Knox Brevard. An unlikely match that not even Ms. Horton had seen coming. Or had she? The woman was more than a second mom. She was all-knowing about everything in Sugar Maple.

Mary-Beth bolted, leaving only Carissa to continue the inquisition. "Are you really going to hire Declan? I mean, aren't you worried about him stealing from you?"

"No." Felicia glanced over her shoulder to discover Declan had vanished. "Listen, I don't know why he did it or if he even committed the crime at all."

"If he went to jail..." Carissa said, insinuating that every person who served time was guilty as charged.

"Do you remember when Stella was accused of graffitiing something and it turned out she was innocent?" Felicia reminded her, as if an indiscretion by a fourteen-year-old girl measured the same as a grown man embezzling money. "And my father? How many times was he picked up for some erroneous reason until my parents finally up and left Sugar Maple?"

"You really think he's innocent, don't you? Did you ask him?"

"I did." Felicia adjusted her apron.

"What did he say?" Carissa tilted her head with that you-better-tell-me-now look.

"He didn't. Actually, he said he wouldn't take the job and that he wouldn't answer the question."

Carissa's expression softened. Her gaze traveled behind Felicia, telling her that Declan had reappeared and was approaching. "That's suspicious, don't you think?"

Felicia explained what Declan had said about why he wouldn't work for her and his answer to the question about the reason for his incarceration.

"That actually makes sense, but do you really think he's trustworthy?" Carissa shifted between feet. "You have a tendency to pick up a lot of pets and people in need. You can't save everyone, you know."

"Did you ever think maybe I need him to save me? I'm desperate for help, and let's face it, Lacey has been anything but a model employee. Declan loaded his camper with all the plants in a fraction of the time it would've taken me. This is my busiest time of year. Add to it this event, the show, and my grandmother... I can't do it all on my own. All the teenagers are still in school, and anyone else worth hiring doesn't want to work outside getting dirty or already has a job."

"Okay. I get it." Carissa took Felicia's hand. "Listen, girl, if you need help, I'm sure we can have a town day or an intervention to help."

"No way. This isn't a case of need like when we refurbished Jake's yard to help him grieve and go back to life after the death of his mother. It's my company, and I need to hire a good employee. One who actually shows up and works."

"You mean like that?" Carissa pointed toward where they'd left the camper.

Declan approached, carrying a lumberjack load of plants. The man was breathtakingly strong. Felicia had always had a soft spot for strong, hard-working men. "Yes."

Declan set the load down and clapped his hands together to rid them of dirt. "You can start organizing while I unload, and then I'll help with whatever you need. As long as I'm not the one decorating. I have no creative abilities."

"You ain't got no abilities." Davey pushed from the bench. After a little wobble, he found his footing and glowered at

Declan. "You best get out of my town. No place here for a bum."

"Hush up now, Davey. You need to be polite. Besides, Declan's not a bum." Carissa flashed a brilliant smile at them all. "He's working for Felicia now."

Felicia blinked at her but then cleared her throat and stood tall. "That's right, he is."

Declan approached with a concerned, shy, chin-lowered kind of look. "I thought we discussed this. You need the right man for the job."

"I think she found him. Look." Carissa pointed at all the plants he'd unloaded. "Besides, she's desperate."

Felicia snapped a narrow-eyed gaze at her.

"I mean, she has a bad employee who isn't helping but getting paid while Felicia is drowning in work. If we don't get her some help soon, she's going to collapse from exhaustion. You wouldn't want that, would you?"

"No, of course not." Declan shoved his hands into his worn jeans pocket and rocked back on his heels. "I'll help you out until you find someone."

"Nope, that's not a job. You need real employment," Davey chimed in with the authority of a supreme court judge. "You work, or you leave. No respect for bums 'round here."

"Okay, I surrender." Declan removed his hands from his pockets and held them up. "I better get moving if I want to prove myself worthy of this job offer. But you still can't pay me for today. I'm only helping a friend out. Deal?" He offered his hand.

She shook it, noticing how his fingers wrapped around her tiny hand, strong yet with a gentleness. "Deal."

"It would be, but a man can't work if he don't have a home. And he can't park that camper at the store no more. Sheriff'll tow it." Davey shuffled away. "Thought you'd outsmarted me. Ha."

Declan's bright eyes fogged with worry. "I can't afford a place right now."

"I can advance you the money."

"No. Not going to happen." Declan backed away, retreating from her and the job opportunity. "Best finish unloading if I'm going to make it to somewhere I can park the camper before tonight."

Carissa patted Felicia's shoulder. "Maybe it's for the best. I mean, I know he's hot and all, but I'd hate to see you get hurt. I trust your judgment, but I'm not the only one you have to convince. The town wouldn't be too happy knowing you had him working out there alone with you all day."

The town had gossiped for weeks when her last boyfriend's car was at her house for two days. They never bothered to find out it was left there so she could take him to the airport for some business meeting up north. The so-called perfect boyfriend material didn't bother to tell her the business meeting was actually a hotel visit with a married woman and the only reason he needed a ride was so that the husband didn't follow him to their rendezvous. Her words filtered in and settled around the only option that could solve both Declan's and her problems, but the town would be in an uproar. "Wait. You can park your camper at the nursery. There's plenty of room. There's even a hookup from when we had a camper ourselves."

Carissa squeezed her shoulder, as if warning her to retract her offer, but she wouldn't. She'd spent too many years making sure everyone else was happy and got along. For once, she was going to choose what was best for herself, and she needed the help. Even if the entire town thought she'd gone pick-up-stray crazy.

FOUR

The fresh spring air turned stale with the realization everyone around Declan stood glaring judgment. "I can't park my camper on your property."

"Why not?" Felicia took one of the potted plants and headed for the gazebo as if she didn't care what he had to say.

He charged after her but with soft steps so as to not look aggressive in front of the town residents. He'd learned years ago that his size and stature made people intimidated and quick to assume the worst about him. She couldn't be this naïve. She had to realize what this would do to her reputation. But was the legend of her kindness to all around her what caused her to sacrifice herself for someone else's needs? "Listen, I know you're a nice person and you're only trying to help, but this isn't a good idea."

"Why?" She didn't even bother to look at him, which aggravated him further.

"Because in case you haven't noticed, the entire town wants me gone. I'm surprised the sheriff hasn't arrived to take me away in handcuffs yet."

Felicia placed the plant in the heart of a circle of flowers already staged next to the white lattice work on the side of the gazebo. "You mean the sheriff headed this way?"

He looked up to indeed find the sheriff marching toward them. "I don't need any trouble. I'm on probation. I'm leaving now." Declan followed the winding path around the flowers toward his camper.

"Hold up." Felicia caught his sleeve, stopping him before he reached the yellow sunflowers near the bench. "Relax. The sheriff's here for part of the Knox Brevard show. I didn't mean to frighten you away. Listen, I get it. You don't want to have any issues here in town with anyone because you accepted the job. If I get the town's approval, will you agree?"

He hadn't noticed the circles under her eyes until now. Was she really that desperate for help? Was Felicia caring for her grandmother on her own? He knew how much of a strain that could be. Add a business to run, and he was surprised she was still on her feet with a smile.

Her gaze traveled his face, as if inspecting every line. The sun reflected in her dark pupils, the color he could only describe as the Petunia Deep Midnight flower she'd showed him earlier but surrounded by a silver pool with yellow glitter flecks scattered like gold dust. Despite his draw to her, he knew he had to refuse. This was all too complicated. His parole officer would tell him to stay away from anything that could damage his freedom. "I don't know. I can't risk getting arrested because Davey reports me for loitering."

"I'll get the sheriff on board, too. Come on." Felicia took his hand, making him feel like he'd jump out of his work boots. The way her heat traveled into his palm, through his wrist, and up his forearm didn't surprise him, but it frightened him. His four-year relationship with his ex-fiancée had ended before the cell door had clanked shut. That was over two years ago.

"Ms. Horton. Over here." Felicia waved with her free hand.

He thought about pulling away, to stop her from this madness, but he couldn't bring himself to let her go, despite his brain screaming at him to run far from this town and Felicia.

"Hi, Felicia. Big day for you?" Ms. Horton, the mayor of Sugar Maple, was dressed in a silver straight skirt with matching jacket and square heels. Even with her sunglasses on, she looked all business.

"I'm good."

To his disappointment, Felicia slipped away to hug Ms. Horton. "You remember Declan, right?"

"Yes, nice to see you again."

Declan nodded his agreement but didn't have time to open his mouth for a proper greeting before Felicia dove into her argument.

"Listen, Davey is being...well, Davey. He's all but chased poor Declan out of town."

"But you want him to stay?" A brow rose over the rim of the dark-brown glasses.

"Yes, I'm desperate for him to. I need help. Look at this place, and with the show, the fact that it's spring, my grandmother, and everything else, I need to hire someone who can actually take a load off my shoulders. And I mean that literally. Declan can help with all the heavy lifting, deliveries, planting, and more."

"You do need help." Ms. Horton's eyes didn't need to be seen for Declan to figure out she was analyzing him from head to toe, assessing his worth and credibility to be near Felicia.

Declan held his breath, not sure if he wanted to run away or beg to stay. His head spun with indecision.

"Then he should work for you." Ms. Horton tugged Felicia into her side. "Unlike the rest of this town, I trust your judgment."

"Thanks. Listen, we've got to go finish unloading, and I need to talk to the sheriff."

"The sheriff? What on earth for?"

Declan opened his mouth to explain Felicia's insane plan, but the minute her fingers slipped between his again, he was lost. Ms. Horton didn't chase after them, so apparently it was a rhetorical question. Like a little puppy, Felicia guided him to the curb where the broken-down senior bus sat. "Sheriff, do you have a minute?"

"Sure thing. What ya need?"

"Davey says its illegal for Declan to park his camper behind the general store."

"He's got a point. I think the town's uneasy and worried about how it looks."

"So he needs to move it?"

"Preferably before tonight, yes." The sheriff adjusted his Texas-style hat.

"Okay. Is it legal to park it on private property with owner's approval if it doesn't show on the main streets?"

"Sure. That's fine."

"Great." Felicia squeezed Declan's fingers, and that's when the sheriff obviously noticed their hand holding, given his raised eyebrow and pointed expression. "Let's get the camper unloaded, and then we can get you settled next to the house at that hook-up I told you about."

Declan eyed the sheriff, the townspeople, the mayor, Felicia's friends and neighbors and knew he had to stop this. He dug in and stood when she tugged him toward the camper. She stumbled forward, her hand slipping from his. "This isn't right. I can't—"

Felicia faced him with a determined look he hadn't seen from her before. "Nope. No way. You made a deal, and you can't renege or people will think you're dishonest."

FIVE

With the last of the plants reloaded into the camper once the filming was over and the sun setting over the Blue Ridge Mountains in the distance, Felicia looked forward to getting Declan settled. Although, she wasn't positive he wouldn't sneak away in the night to avoid trouble. She needed to make him feel more welcome than the town had so far.

"Thanks so much for your help today. I seriously couldn't have pulled this off without you." Felicia eyed the back of his camper. "And it doesn't appear as if too much soil spilled out onto your carpet. I'll vacuum it out for you when we get home."

"No way. You show me where you keep your cleaning supplies, and I'll take care of it before I leave."

The way he casually mentioned leaving didn't escape her notice. He was digging his heels in and turning onto the road headed out of town. "Then after you're done, you need to come inside for dinner. I won't take no for an answer."

"I can't," he said in a hoarse whisper.

"You'll be doing me a favor. Since there's no home nurse on the weekends, Nana has been alone all day except for Ms. Horton stopping in to check on her while I was working. She needs some company while I cook and clean up. Seriously, you'd be doing me a huge favor."

He stared at the road ahead, as if contemplating the political turmoil of the nation instead of accepting a meal invitation. "Sure. I'm happy to help." He offered a sad grin and said, "I know what it's like to care for a loved one who's aging. My mother has dementia."

"I'm so sorry." A knot formed in Felicia's chest at the way Declan's eyes hooded and his mouth went slack. "I know you love her based on the way Stella's father used it to get you to bring him here. How is she now?"

"Gone mentally, except for patches of clarity. Unfortunately, those patches lead to her yelling and spewing hatred toward me." His hands gripped the steering wheel a little tighter than necessary to turn onto the driveway.

"It's tough watching the ones we love deteriorate in front of our eyes. Some days I long for the grandmother who would kneel by my side in the garden. I love the quiet of working in a field or flower bed, but it can get lonely without her next to me." Felicia pointed to the split in the drive that led around the back of the house. "Pull around here. There's an actual hook-up out back. My parents had a motor home years ago. I don't know if it all still works, but if it does you can use it."

His expression lit up. "Thanks. I've been showering in truck stops. It'll be nice to at least camp shower in here."

"No need. There's a shower in the house."

He turned onto the pad at the other side of the house and stopped a little too abruptly, sending her against the seat belt. "I need to make sure you understand that I'll pay rent for this spot once I've earned my way here—or you can deduct it from my pay—but I won't use anything inside. I'm fine with what I have, and it wouldn't be appropriate for me to use your shower each day. I'm a tenant."

Felicia didn't like the way he put up a retaining wall each time she tried to give him a little help. If she was being honest with herself, it felt like a personal rejection. Perhaps he wanted to make it clear he didn't like her as more than a friend. "Water and utilities are included with the rent, as is the use of the facilities if you so choose to use them." She hopped out and headed for the door, eager to check on her grandmother.

Declan cut her off at the back of the camper. "Wait. I'm sorry. I can tell that I've hurt your feelings, and that isn't what I intended. Listen, you're the nicest person I've ever met. The only person who's treated me like a human being since I was released, but I can't take advantage of your kindness. This isn't personal. I need to maintain a positive environment where I can concentrate on my future with as few complications as possible. I'm under probation, which means no alcohol, no theft, not anything. If I were to have access to your home and there's beer, I could get in trouble. If something went missing and I have access inside, then I'll be blamed, and that could mean returning to jail. I will not allow myself to return to that place."

His voice cracked, and she knew he'd suffered greatly. "I'm sorry. I never thought of it that way. That was selfish of me. I only wanted some company for my grandmother and to keep you here to help with the work. I'm afraid I resorted to manipulation with material things to entice you not to flee in the night, leaving me here with more work than I can handle."

He tilted her chin up to look at him. The man was tall and wide as a beast but with the touch of a lightning bug in the night. "You could never be selfish." His breath sounded short and quick. "It's more than just the alcohol and the theft. It's you."

He stepped away and cleared his throat before she could gather her wits and ask what he meant. "I'm going to clean up, and then I'll go knock on the front door in about twenty minutes. I'd be honored to sit with your grandmother while you get some rest."

"Wait, what did you mean?" she blurted, as if her lips finally caught up to her imagination. Her heart beat faster than hummingbird wings flapping.

"You're an extremely attractive woman. A kind, gentle, giving, talented woman who deserves better than an ex-con. I won't allow myself to complicate your life more than it already is." He ran a hand through his thick hair that fell above his eyebrows. "I'll make a deal with you. I'll help out any way I can, including with your grandmother, as long as we maintain a friendly business relationship in which we're never alone inside the house."

"But—"

"You want me to stay? That's the condition."

"Can I ask why?" Felicia studied the moon rising into the sky. "Did I do something to make you uncomfortable?"

"No, not in any way. You're perfect." He laced his fingers behind his head and turned to face the open field. "I don't trust myself. Please, just agree."

The desperation in his voice, as if he waged an internal war between good and evil, made her realize if she wanted the help and to keep Declan around until she could show him he was worth more than just self-loathing and hiding from the world, she'd have to agree.

"Fine. I'll see you in twenty. In the morning, I start at sunrise."

He dropped his hands to his sides. "See you in twenty."

Felicia headed to the edge of the house before he shouted after her.

"Wait."

She paused, expecting him to soften and say he was sorry for making her feel so dejected.

"One more thing." Declan faced her. Even in the dimming light, she could see his set jaw. "You have to lock your doors at night. There needs to be no doubt that I can't enter your house at any point unsupervised."

The way his voice dipped to a warning tone sent a shiver through her. For the first time since they'd met, she doubted that this man was the saint she thought he was, an angel sent to help and to give her comfort. Maybe he was still an angel but a dark one.

SIX

Declan hooked up the water to the house and took a camp shower from his wet room. One appendage at a time since his shoulders didn't fit inside the tiny space. He longed to go inside Felicia's home and explain why he'd said those things to her about keeping the doors locked and him out of her life. There was an awkwardness between them now that he didn't like. The way she bolted inside with a dark, downturned gaze after their conversation made him want to explain why he made such demands. But she'd only argue with him, and his words were necessary to put a wedge between them. If he didn't, his growing attraction for her would become too great for him to deny, and she deserved better than him. She deserved the world.

He put on a clean shirt and brushed his unruly hair, took a deep breath, and headed to the front door. For a moment, he wished he had flowers in his hand to show her how much she meant to him for helping him out, but that wouldn't be appropriate. Besides, the woman could grow her own. If he were to bring a gift as if they were on a date, he'd come up with something far better.

The front door creaked open, and Felicia stepped aside,

allowing plenty of space for him to enter. She'd never been so distant before. Inside he found the place clean and tidy with an older décor that probably housed Felicia's grandmother's belongings more than her own. Something told him that Felicia never required much to be happy. She had a servant's heart. One that he desired for himself but knew he'd never achieve in his lifetime.

Felicia's grandmother sat asleep in a reclining chair facing an old television with reruns of a black and white show playing. Felicia paused at her side and looked down as if debating about waking her. "She'll probably sleep while I cook. I'll wake her for dinner."

"Let me help." He headed for the kitchen. Once, in a past life, he'd enjoyed cooking and baking. He'd started preparing all the meals the first time his mother had forgotten to turn off the stove, and over time he'd found it a stress reliever in his life. Creating something instead of having something torn apart like his life had been.

Felicia straggled in behind him. "You don't have to. You're my guest."

"Nope. I'm your tenant who can't pay. I'd like to make dinner for you and your grandmother as a thank-you."

"You've already thanked me enough by working all day."

"That paid for my room for the night. Now I'm paying you for the water and food I'm consuming."

Felicia huffed. "Fine, but why can't you just accept a friendly gesture and stop turning everything into a business arrangement?" She opened the refrigerator and tossed some chicken onto the counter. "I know what you were doing outside, and you need to stop."

He opened a cupboard and snagged a few ingredients he thought could dress up the chicken and found some arborio rice and vegetable stock to make risotto as the side. She also retrieved broccoli and set it on the counter next to the chicken. "I don't know what you mean."

Before he realized what was happening, she slid herself between him and the counter, leaving only inches between them. He dropped the rice and vegetable stock to the floor. The can rolled across the tile, only stopping when it hit the carpet threshold to the living room. He couldn't speak, couldn't breathe for several seconds.

"You listen to me. I know you want to make sure you protect yourself from any issues that could harm your parole, and I completely understand that, but the deranged way you said it was intended to scare me. Well, it didn't work. I'm not and never will be scared of you, Declan Mills, so get over yourself and stop pushing me away. I won't hurt you. I've been thinking, and I'm guessing you didn't even commit the crime you served time for. I can't reconcile the man in front of me with a criminal. Perhaps you went to jail because of some plea deal, or covering for someone else, or you were reformed. I don't know which, and I don't care. You're a good and caring man. I'm sorry you're so scared of me that you push me away, but I'm a good person too. You don't have to worry about me causing you further harm. I could never hurt you."

"I didn't mean to make you feel like I didn't trust you." He couldn't resist touching her tight cheek at the sight of her wounded gaze. She relaxed into his hand but remained with straight posture and eyes wide, as if to drive her point home that she wouldn't back down. He'd never met a stronger person, not even while incarcerated.

For several moments they only stood, staring at each other as if having a discussion without words.

"I hate to point out the obvious, but you have nowhere else to go, and I think you could be happy here. I'm not putting you down in any way because I know you could make it anywhere, but I need you as much as you need me."

He couldn't help but feel like she was talking about more than just a job right now. It had to be lonely out here, and more than anything he knew how lonely it was to care for a person who was once your parental figure. That's when he saw it... Felicia, despite all the people in town and her best friends since childhood, still needed a friend. A good friend who wasn't distracted by his or her own life. "You're right."

She blinked, as if surprised she didn't have to fight more.

"About most of it. I did push you away and try to frighten you so that I could protect myself from any trouble. And let's face it, feelings are trouble. And Felicia, I have feelings for you, the kind that mean I want to take you on a date, bring you presents, hold your hand, and watch the sunset or the night stars."

She leaned into him, and he knew there still had to be a line drawn between them. He had to find the strength to control his own emotions and desires. "But that can never be." He dropped his hand to his side and backed away. The distance was like a mile-deep crevasse between them he feared he'd fall into if he touched her again.

"Why?" she whispered, as if she didn't want to know the truth.

Declan hunted for a pot, for a knife, for the pepper, for anything but Felicia and her distracting pull. "You need to promise me that if I stay here, we keep things platonic. I'd love to be your friend and live here while I get on my feet and help you, but I can't get close to you."

"Not that I'm saying I want any more than a friendship with you... Yes, I like and respect you. You're the hardest worker I know. But why close off possibilities? You just said you like me, so I don't understand."

He forced his emotions under control, knowing she would argue with any reason he gave, leaving them both open to complications between them. And he couldn't let that thought exist. "You don't have to. You just have to respect my wishes." He pushed his shoulders back and hand out to her. "Deal?"

Her lips pressed into a thin line, and her brows furrowed. He could see the internal struggle rage inside her, but then she took his hand with a firm grip. "Deal."

Relief should have flooded him, but her touch only doused him with more doubt, opening him up to *what ifs*, so he slipped away under the guise of preparing the chicken for dinner.

Felicia cleared her throat. "For now, until you see yourself the way I see you. A man worthy of more than just a job. A man worthy of compassion, companionship, and to be cherished for all the gifts he offers the world."

SEVEN

Dinner tasted even more amazing than it smelled. Felicia dug in, and to her surprise, Nana used her adapted fork to puncture a piece and ate it in front of a stranger. The same Nana who refused to eat in front of anyone but Felicia.

Fluffy and Fuzzy meowed at their feet, as if the aroma was feline fabulous, too. Nana managed to eat five pieces before her arm gave out and she dropped the fork to the table.

Declan retrieved the utensil before she could warn him that Nana might impale him with it. "Let me help you with that."

Instead of Nana chomping her mouth shut like a vise grip, she opened wide. She chewed the piece while Declan arranged the strap on her other hand. "I know it'll be tough, and you need to use the other arm as much as possible, but let's try using your nondominant hand for part of the meal."

Nana swallowed. "I don't know if I can. The therapist tried to get me to last time I saw her, and I nearly poked my eye out."

"What if I keep my hand on yours and guide it to your mouth?" Declan asked in a non-condescending, I'm-happy-to-help tone.

She smiled. *Nana smiled.* What was going on? Felicia had

tried to get Nana to try the other hand every day, but she'd given up the last time after her grandmother threw her plate on the floor and refused to ever eat again. "I think I can do it if you help me."

Felicia sat back and watched as her fiercely independent grandmother melted into whatever Declan said. That was his gift—helping people without making them feel like they needed assistance. As if it was his absolute pleasure with no strings attached. This was not the personality of a bad man who served time, white collar or not. A man like this didn't take what didn't belong to him. He only knew how to give.

"You gonna sit there staring at me throughout dinner, or you going to eat? Because if you aren't going to eat that, I will."

Felicia picked up her fork but watched out of the corner of her eye as Declan dabbed at her grandmother's mouth. The woman was acting like a schoolgirl with a crush, giggling in between bites. She didn't even scream or throw something when food fell from her mouth. Was Nana flirting?

The meal continued until the woman who hadn't eaten more than a few morsels of a meal since her stroke had cleaned her plate. Felicia savored the last two bites of rich goodness on her own plate. Declan dabbed her grandmother's lips, brushed off the crumbs on her bib, and then unstrapped the fork from her hand. "Next time, we'll try to go a little longer with the other hand, but now you know you can eat with both."

"Only with your help." Nana winked at him.

Felicia dropped her fork unceremoniously onto her plate with a loud clank.

"Don't be jealous. I need the help. You don't," Nana said with a devious chuckle.

Felicia wanted to ask what the heck was going on, but she'd wait until later when they were alone. "I'll get these dishes done."

"I've got them. You hang with your grandmother while I clean up."

"You cooked," Felicia said, stacking her plate on his.

Declan swiped all three plates and stood. "You've had a long day, and I've been monopolizing your lovely nana all through dinner. I'll let you two have some time together." He reached the sink and started the water before she could argue. Which was fine with her because she couldn't hold it in any longer.

"What's going on with you?"

Nana's thin, painted-on brows rose. "Whatever do you mean?"

Felicia leaned over the table and whispered, "You ate all your dinner. You never eat like that."

"You don't cook like that. No offense, darling, but you're a terrible chef." Nana waved her hands at Felicia. "And get your elbows off the table. Have you forgotten your manners?"

She dropped her hands to her lap but kept leaning in to talk without Declan overhearing them. "It's not just that you ate all your food. You were...were...flirting with him."

"I'm old but I ain't blind, not legally anyway."

"What's that supposed to mean?" Felicia asked.

"It means that if you're not going to go after that hunk of handsome, I will." She pursed her lips in a wrinkly O shape.

Felicia sat back in her chair. "It's complicated."

"What's complicated? He's handsome, strong, kindhearted, giving, a hard worker, and has a butt you could bounce a shovel off of."

"Nana."

"What? I'm not lying." She eyed Declan like another piece of his excellently prepared chicken.

Felicia debated how much to tell her grandmother. If she told her the truth, would she insist that he leave? Would she turn on him because he had served time? It didn't matter. This was her grandmother's house, and she deserved to know the truth. In all the years she'd lived with Nana, the number-one rule was that they didn't keep secrets from each other. "He's an ex-con."

The water cut off, and Felicia knew he'd heard her. She wanted to pull the words back in, but it was too late.

"So?" She didn't seem the least bit surprised.

"Wait, you knew?" Felicia crossed her arms over her chest.

"I had a stroke. I'm not deaf." She shrugged. Her left shoulder moved close to her ear, but the other one only rose a millimeter or two. "I do have visitors, you know. I'm not a complete hermit."

"Ms. Horton." Of course she'd told Nana. Ms. Horton always looked out for the girls, and despite the fact that she'd agreed to allow Declan to stay in town, she wouldn't leave Felicia completely unprotected.

"Maybe. Doesn't matter. If you can't see he's a good man, you don't deserve him."

Wow. Where had that come from? "No man I've ever brought home has been good enough for me. But Declan, a man the town wants to drive outside of our boarders, one who served time, is unemployed, is good enough for me?"

Nana let out a long breath and eyed Declan washing dishes behind Felicia. "You know, sometimes the world isn't fair. You of all people should know that. Like you, trying to keep your head high as people judged you because you were created by a mixed couple, he too faces judgment. Yes, you didn't choose the life you were given, but it doesn't mean he's any less worthy of our kindness. You don't have to marry him. Although, I didn't want to say anything, but you're not getting any younger."

"Seriously, I'm not even thirty."

"I know. You'd be a spinster in my day. I was married at sixteen. Of course, I had to run off and marry him without my parents knowing, since he'd been dishonorably discharged from the military. It didn't matter that he was a good man. All people saw was that one blemish on his history."

"I didn't know that about Grandpa." Felicia shook her head. "I thought we didn't keep things from each other."

"Wasn't my story to tell." Nana tried to shrug again. This time, her bad shoulder moved a little higher.

Car lights shone through the front window, drawing Felicia to look out to see who was approaching. Irritation and relief fought for dominance at the sight of her truck approaching. "Great, Lacey's back."

"You gonna fire her?" Nana said with grit in her tone. "That girl's done taken advantage of you long enough."

Fluffy hissed at the door as if agreeing with Nana.

Felicia took a deep breath and forced herself to face the truth that sometimes things had to get ugly before they got better. "No, but I'm going to demote her and let her know she has one last chance."

Lacey didn't have an opportunity to knock on the door before Felicia opened it and stepped aside for her to enter. "Nice of you to return my truck before the sheriff picked you up for auto theft."

Lacey strutted into the middle of the room. "You're so funny. Here's your keys. I know I didn't make it back in time for the town thingy, but it wasn't my fault. The truck conked out on me."

"Really, all the way in Riverbend?"

"What?" Lacey blinked, obviously shocked Felicia already knew the truth. Her eyes did that dance they did when she was trying to concoct a new lie. "I only ran over to pick up some help. I mean, there was no way I could do all that myself today."

"I'm sorry I asked too much of you. You obviously can't handle the responsibilities of the job." Felicia forced an even tone, not allowing herself to waiver. Stella would be proud of her. "Due to that reason, I'm going to demote you to office assistant. Your hours will be cut, and you'll be on thirty days probation."

"That's not fair," Lacey whined. "I need the money."

Lacey wanted to pull her cousin into a hug and tell her it would be okay, but for once she knew being supportive wasn't the answer. She'd tried that already. The perfect, honest, giving, hardworking young girl had changed since her boyfriend had entered her life. "I need someone who will do the work."

"Okay, I'll do better." Lacey dipped her chin to her chest and twirled her hair in her finger. "I'll be here tomorrow morning to help with the planting."

Felicia wanted to believe her words, wanted to help her cousin, wanted the girl she once knew to return instead of this mixed up person that couldn't even show up for work on time. The once dedicated, smart, reliable, vibrant girl had grown into a solemn, unreliable young adult. Felicia mourned the loss of that once true friend. "You're not listening. I can't wait for you to decide to show up sometime in the afternoon when I scheduled you to arrive at dawn."

"I'll be here by nine, I promise."

"No. You'll be here at seven to return phone calls and do office work for a few hours and then leave at two. I've hired someone else to be my right-hand man with all the other work. If this isn't acceptable, there's the door." Felicia's stomach churned, and she regretted eating those last few bites.

"But there aren't any other jobs." Lacey's voice hitched an octave higher, making her sound like a crying child.

"I've tolerated your antics longer than most employers would. It's time for you to grow up. You were once a responsible young woman I found irreplaceable, but now, you're none of those things."

Tears pooled in her eyes. "You can't do this. Mama said if I wasn't in college and didn't keep a job, she'd kick me out."

Felicia wanted to convince Lacey, the girl who took college level classes in high school to go to the university, but she'd refused. Felicia guessed it had less to do with her own wants and desires and more to do with her love for the wrong man. "Then I suggest you be on time tomorrow, or you'll have to find a new job and a new place to live. Do you understand me?" Felicia asked, not expecting her to actually agree.

"If I show you that I'm a hard worker, will you give me more hours?" Lacey asked. This time she actually did look sincere.

"We'll reevaluate after thirty days. That's the best I can offer," Felicia said in a firm tone, despite her insides melting due to nepotism.

That's when Declan arrived in the room, drying his hands on a towel. Lacey turned from sincere to flirtatious, returning to twirling her hair and batting her eyelashes.

"Who's this?" she asked, sauntering over to Declan with a sway to her hips that would make a prostitute look innocent.

"I'm Declan. I was just hired on here to help out. Nice to meet you."

Lacey's hand dropped from her hair, and she glowered at him. "So you're the one who stole my job."

At that moment, Felicia saw the drama about to unfold in her living room, so she attempted to appease Lacey. "Actually, no, I need all the assistance I can get. I've hired Declan to help out with the heavy lifting while you work in the office. We both know you don't like to mess up your manicure."

With only a huff, Lacey stomped out of the house, leaving Felicia unsure if she'd even return tomorrow. A car pulled into the drive. Lacey got in, and the wheels spun gravel before the car sped away.

"Well, that was exhausting," Nana said with a hand to her

brow in a good southern swooning motion. "I'm turning in. Oh, Declan, would you mind helping Felicia with one more thing tonight?"

"I'd be happy to," Declan said, his eyes still planted on the door where Lacey had just run out.

"Great. My television is acting up. Could you take a look at it? It's all an old woman like me has during the long, lonely days here."

Felicia swallowed her guilt and hoped to do better for her grandmother.

"Sure. What's wrong with it?" he asked, eyeing the old set.

"I don't know. You'll have to watch it to find out." Nana retrieved an old DVD from her five-shelf collection and handed it to Declan. "You'll need to watch for about twenty minutes before you'll see the problem." Nana hurried out of the room, leaving Declan and Felicia alone.

Declan rounded the coffee table, as if to put distance between them. "I have a sneaking suspicion there's nothing wrong with the television."

"Why's that?"

Declan handed her the DVD, and in large print on the back, she read, *Innocent ex-con saved by the love of a small-town girl.*

He let out a long breath and ran a hand through his hair. "Something tells me you're not the only person I need to convince that I'm no good for you."

EIGHT

The sun had never looked so beautiful. It rose above the weeping willow at the front of Felicia's property. Declan sat on the roof of his camper and watched the glorious spectacle of tangerine and rose–colored streams in the sky. Not even on the roof of his twelve-story downtown flat had he ever seen anything as beautiful.

This day. A new day filled with opportunity he didn't have yesterday made him appreciate the cool wind drifting through the tree branches of the large maple. He'd parked between the house and the tree where Felicia had instructed. Little did he know at the time that this was the best spot on the property.

Declan sipped his bitter coffee, but he didn't care. Camp beverages were his new norm. No more uppity, overpriced frou-frou café concoctions to start his day. Besides, he'd kicked that habit while incarcerated. It wasn't like anyone made him a latte before he cleaned the dishes and scrubbed the floors.

"Good morning. Can I come up?" Felicia's voice drew his attention to the front walk where she stood in her work pants and crimson t-shirt holding two cups of coffee. "I brought you something, but it looks like you already made your own."

"Oh, I'll take it." He abandoned his mug to the top of the camper next to his seat and shot out of his lawn chair to the ladder. "Pass them up and you can join me. That is, if we have time before work starts. I wasn't sure on the schedule, so I set my alarm for five."

She held up the two cups to him and then climbed to the roof. "Sorry about that. I should've given you specific work hours. I'm not used to Lacey showing before noon, and I'm usually up before anyone else to feed the animals."

"No worries at all. I like to be up early to work out and have some quiet reflection time." Declan took a sip of smooth, caffeinated bliss and unfolded the lawn chair with the broken seat he'd pulled out this morning and directed Felicia to the good one. "I found some dog food, and since the pups were animated I thought it might be feeding time, so I gave them a scoop from the bag and took the bucket I thought was slop to the pig. The donkey hasn't been fed yet. I wasn't sure what he ate."

"Wow, you're a hard worker. I'm sure Petunia, our pig, appreciated you feeding her early. She gets cranky if I feed her too late. Our donkey, Donald, isn't so picky." She looked around for a moment at the view atop of the camper. "I'll let you enjoy your break. I didn't mean to interrupt." Felicia took a step toward the ladder.

Despite not wanting to get close to Felicia romantically, her company was a divine gift and he didn't want to let it go yet. "You're not bothering me at all, really," he said in a tone he could only describe as desperate for her to stay. He cleared his throat. "I wouldn't want you to miss this sunrise."

She glanced over her shoulder and then sat down in the indicated lawn chair and lifted her coffee to rest it in her hands with the brim under her nose. "You make it sound like the best sunrise ever." Her hair wasn't pulled back like it had been when he'd seen her working. The long strands were shiny and framed her high cheekbones, but when she glanced down into her cup and the hair fell over her face, he longed to pull it back so he could see her beautiful eyes.

"It is. Look." He pointed at the mountains on the horizon. "The colors are vibrant." He took a sip of his coffee, a much better concoction than what he'd made with instant grounds and barely hot water.

She leaned back in the chair and watched the sun rise a little higher, taking a sip of her coffee every so often. "I didn't know how you liked your coffee," she said after a moment. "I can go get some cream and sugar for you if you like."

"No, this is perfect. I'm used to bitter and old, so this is a far improvement from my norm."

They sat only inches apart, but it was a safe enough distance for him to realize he didn't need to keep a ten-foot wall up between them. Perhaps a three-foot space would do. Certainly that was a safe distance for physical attraction.

They needed a friendship, one that was pleasant but not too intimate. After all, he'd be working with her for however long she'd keep him on. This would be good when he reported to his parole officer next week.

"How's your grandmother this morning? I was going to go in and make breakfast for you both, but I decided not to intrude. Perhaps if we set up a schedule, I could make the meals. If you give me a time that you're up and can let me inside."

"I'm not paying you to make meals. No need to feel like you have to do more than your job."

"I want to. I like to stay busy. Not much to do hanging in a camper all evening. I mean, I read when I have a good book, exercise, and such."

"That's how you stay so fit." She swept her hair behind her shoulder, revealing a tinge of pink on her face. "I mean, you stay in shape."

"I try." He wanted to tell her the same. That working in a nursery was obviously keeping her small, curvy figure perfect, but that would make things more awkward. He needed this job, so he needed to keep his focus on what was important. Not on the exotically beautiful, kind-hearted woman like none other he'd met prior. He'd found one or the other quality in women before but not a combination of them both. "We should get to work. I don't want to sit around when I can be helping. What needs to get done first? And don't go easy on me. You can't scare me off."

"Not with hard labor anyway." Her remark settled in the air between them like an elephant in ballet slippers wearing a fuchsia tutu.

"Felicia." He closed his eyes, battling between wanting to make her smile and wanting to protect her from the life he'd fallen into. "I-I didn't mean to offend you in any way."

"Relax. Let's get to work." She shot up and headed for the ladder, but he sensed her irritation and he didn't like it.

He snagged her arm but let go just as quickly. The words he wanted to say, the compliments, the endearments, the affection all trapped in his throat, and they were better off for that. "You're right. We need to get to work."

There were no other words between them until they got to work. In fact, they barely spoke all morning except for Felicia directing him where to move the bags of soil and mulch. How to prune a bush and when to water which plant.

The silence nearly drove him to confess his attraction before an olive green car came charging down the front drive. It slid to a halt, and Lacey hopped out of the passenger side before the driver sped off once more. Declan glanced at his watch to see she was over five hours late.

She sauntered up to where Felicia was on her knees trans-ferring plants from containers to the field. Declan wanted to march over and tell the girl she was taking advantage of a kind woman, but he kept his nose down and focused on irrigating the new lines Felicia would be planting tomorrow.

"You're late," Felicia said in a tone Declan hadn't heard before out of her.

"I'm not late. You said that I wouldn't be doing anything but office work, and you work outside all morning." Lacey looked down at her impractical heeled sandals and then at Felicia as if her attire explained everything.

"I told you to be here at seven. It's now after noon. Go home. Return when you're ready to work at the time I tell you to work. If not, don't come back." Felicia continued to tug weeds from the ground and didn't even give Lacey a sideways glance. But the way her shoulders were near her ears and her arms were tense told Declan she struggled with saying these things.

"I can't leave. I don't have a ride. And you know my cell doesn't work out here in the sticks." Lacey said that as if she was above even standing on the dirty ground beneath her. "I guess I'll take the truck."

"No, you'll go in the house and call your boyfriend to come get you. He can't be that far away yet."

Lacey huffed. "You serious? He has things to do. He's not going to come get me right now."

Felicia set her small shovel down and wiped her brow. "That should tell you something about your choice in boyfriends."

"You've never liked him. That's what this is about." Lacey squared herself into a fighting stance in front of Felicia.

Declan stood on the sidelines, wanting to run interference.

"If your boyfriend won't return for you, then call your mother." She looked up at Lacey in a way that brooked no room for an argument.

Lacey spun toward the house with a double huff and

marched across the lawn, not even careful to mind the flowers planted along the front walk. Declan wanted to escort her off the property like he had in his college bouncer days.

The way Felicia sat with her palms pressed to her thighs and her head down told him it wasn't natural for her to be that direct, but she wouldn't let people walk all over her. She was a good woman. "You did the right thing," he mumbled but kept his attention on retrieving another bag of soil, opening it, and pouring it into the pre-dug holes.

"I know. It doesn't make it any easier. Sometimes we have to work hard to maintain boundaries, even when they're not easy."

"Why don't you just fire her for good?" Declan blurted before he remembered it wasn't his place to ask.

"Because sometimes the boundaries that are hardest to establish are the ones worth the most effort. That young girl has been through a lot, and she's a wiz with numbers. She's strong and smart and was by my side after my grandmother had her stroke. Without her, this place would've gone under. I'm not good with the books." She removed a glove, wiped her brown and tossed a glance at the front of the house. "Her biggest fault is in her choice of men. One man, actually. I hate to see her waste her life. That being said, it's ultimately her decision. She's eighteen now, and it's time for her to take responsibility."

He couldn't help but think there was a deeper meaning to her words. Was she talking about their boundaries as worker and boss being more, or was it wishful thinking, despite what he knew to be the right decision?

She kept eyeing the front door, and he knew she was worried about Lacey inside. "Tell you what. I'd like to whip up some lunch for you and your mother. Since I'm done with this row, why don't I go get started? I'll wash up and make some pressed sandwiches. Sound good?"

"Sounds delicious. I usually eat some carrots or some chips to tide me over until dinner."

He dumped the remaining soil out of the bag, rolled up the plastic, and placed it in the recycling bin. "Not while I'm around. As long as I'm here, you'll be well taken care of." The words slipped out before he realized what he'd said, but instead of making it more awkward by trying to explain what he'd meant, he went inside the house to find Lacey digging through a drawer at the desk next to the kitchen. "What're you doing?"

"None of your business." Lacey shut the drawer with a loud bang. "I know what you're doing. And I won't let you."

"What am I doing?" he asked, crossing the living room, not even caring if he intimidated the young lady with his size and odor after working in the heat all morning.

"You're stealing my job and the woman who looks after me. Well, I found out in town about your sordid history. I'll tell Felicia all about your jail time."

He lifted his chin, not even giving her a chance to expand on her devious plans. "She knows. Everything."

Lacey's face scrunched like the truth gave her a headache. "I don't believe you." Her lips curved into a mischievous, all-knowing grin. "Oh, wait, you're her newest stray. Well, you might stay here for a while, but once you steal from her, you'll be out." Lacey waltzed up to him with hands on her hips, not even the least bit shy.

He didn't back down. "I would never steal from anyone here in Sugar Maple or anywhere else."

"You don't actually have to steal. They just have to *believe* you did." Lacey poked a finger to his chest. "You better get lost, or you'll be back in jail."

NINE

Felicia bolted upright at four in the morning. "Dear Lord. I can't believe I forgot." She shot out of bed, threw on her clothes, and with flashlight in hand, she walked the grounds.

In all the craziness of the filming, deliveries, planting, she'd forgotten about the floral arrangements for Ms. Horton to see today. The woman who'd done everything for her, including stopping in often to check on Nana when Felicia was out all day working.

Bugs of all shapes and sizes flew into the beam of light shining at the plants on the front walk. In her head she'd been working on these arrangements for weeks, but she hadn't put them together. Now, she only had a few hours to get them ready.

She stumbled along the walkway, hunting for the good shears. Her toe connected with a metal bucket, sending it tumbling down the cement steps with a clang and a clatter of tools. Felicia froze and held her breath, willing her nana and Declan not to wake up, but it didn't work.

Sergeant, Mack, and Troop all barked from the kennel. The light inside the camper flicked on, and rapid footsteps pounded.

She scurried to pick up the tools and dropped the flashlight, which rolled down the steps, sending beams of light in all directions.

The door flew open and slammed against the side of the camper. "Who's there?"

"Sorry, it's me," she shouted, thinking Declan would be pouncing on any intruder. The man was all protection and old-school gentleman when it came to women, even though he seemed to value them as equals.

"You all right? What's going on?" He shuffled into the dimly lit front yard to her side.

"Nothing. I was trying to work, and I kicked over a bucket. Go back to bed." Felicia found the bucket between the rose bushes and set it upright.

"Working? It's four something in the morning." Declan knelt and retrieved some of the tools scattered around him.

The flashlight shone white across his body. The toned, well-developed, and tan body dressed in nothing but boxer shorts. Felicia dropped the hand shovel with the loudest clank she'd ever heard. She snatched it up and dropped it into the bucket. "Right. Um...yeah, I know." She retrieved the shears, keeping her gaze carefully toward the ground. "Inspiration and all."

"You're inspired at this hour?"

She stole a sideways glance at the statue of perfection at her side. "Yep. You never know when and where inspiration will strike." Great... She sounded breathless and wanting.

He caught her looking at him and smiled. A sexy smile that was like a shining exclamation point to all that was distracting about him.

She cleared her throat and shot up, only to hit her head on his chin and fall back, leaving them both rubbing their bruises. "Sorry."

"No need to be." He stood, adjusting the cuff of his boxers

around his thighs, which only drew her attention for a second before she forced herself to move away and analyze the rose bush. "I'll go put some clothes on. I wouldn't normally greet you in this condition, but I thought there was someone breaking into your home. I came running without thinking."

"I'm glad you did." Heat flooded her face. "I mean, it's good to know you're here if anything ever did happen." She forced her hand from her head despite the throbbing and attacked the stem of a rose with the wrong shears, only shredding it instead of a clean cut. "I better go find the right tool for this job."

"Your favorite ones are on the workbench in the office. I hope you don't mind, but I was a little bored last night, so I arranged your tools and put together the corkboard and hooks you had in the box next to the bench."

"Oh, thanks. You don't have to work after hours, though. Please, go back to sleep. Actually, take the morning off. I need to work on a project and deliver it to town, so I won't need you before lunch."

"I'd like to help if you don't mind. As a friend, I mean. I can work later." He backed away. "Let me go throw on some clothes. I'll meet you in the office."

"No. You don't have to help," she called after him, but he didn't stop. Instead, the camper rocked with his weight entering, and then she saw him opening a drawer through the window. This time, she tore her gaze away and kept it on her work, fleeing to the office far from the distracting, half-dressed body of perfection.

To her amazement, he'd organized everything. Something she'd asked Lacey to do months ago. The boxes of tools were hung on the wall. Planters were cleaned and stacked. The floor was swept, and even the desk papers were organized. She retrieved the correct shears and headed outside, only to run smack into Declan's hard chest. She backed away, but not before she caught a whiff of his woodsy, outdoorsman scent that had to be his deodorant—or he naturally smelled that good first thing in the morning.

"Where do we start?" he asked with a cheer in his voice she didn't expect at this ungodly hour of the day.

"We need to cut the flowers and then bring them in here to put together into arrangements. I need to have a centerpiece, bridal bouquet, and one example of a bridesmaid bouquet. It'll be a good enough sample to see what I have to offer. We'll be choosing dark-color roses and I think light-color lilies as a contrast. I'll also select some appropriate greenery and filler plants."

"Sounds nice." He went to the workbench and found another set of shears and a basket and then walked toward the front garden as if he knew what to do based on her instructions.

Lacey would've stood next to her and held the basket. She jogged to catch up to an eager Declan and settled by his side at the rose bushes.

"I think these would be perfect." Declan pointed to the deep-colored flowers with wine and purple accents.

"Yes, they will be." She analyzed the blooms with her flash-light and found a perfectly opened rose.

"Here, let me hold that for you so you can show me the proper way to cut one." He covered her hand with his. His large fingers wrapped around in a comforting touch. She relinquished the light and forced a calming breath so she didn't do anything stupid, like try to keep hold of him after he'd made it clear there would never be anything between them. It had been a long time since a man turned her head, but she wouldn't go after someone who wasn't interested. Although, she had a hint or two he was.

"You grab the stem halfway down; that way you leave

enough leaves below so that a new flower will grow quicker than if you cut it too low." She demonstrated and then handed the flower to him.

He inhaled a deep breath with the petals to his nose. She must've looked at him with a questioning look, because he placed the flower in the basket and said, "No better time to stop and smell the roses than in the early morning hours before your day begins."

"How are you so optimistic, considering what you've been through over the last few years?" She cut another stem and passed it to him.

He placed the basket on the ground and pulled the shears from his pocket. "Those last few years were what made me appreciate today. There's no better life than this."

She shrugged, but apparently he didn't like her response, because he set his shears and flower in the basket and took her by her shoulders. "Close your eyes."

"What? No. I have work to do." She didn't sound too convincing, but how could she, with this man so close to her, distracting her from the task at hand?

"Humor me. I promise that I'll help you finish before you have to take these."

Somehow she doubted a man who looked like him, a protector and comforter type, would know how to arrange flowers, but if she wanted to get back to work, she needed to humor him. "Fine." She closed her eyes.

"Now listen."

She did as instructed, and she heard crickets chirping a song all around them. A distant howl from an animal. The soft tapping of the wind vane in the backyard. How had she not noticed them before now?

"What do you hear?"

"Insects, animals."

"The song of the morning welcoming you," he breathed. His warm breath grazed her cheek, and her body awoke. It no longer felt like the middle of the night but as if a vibrant sunrise crested the mountains.

For several seconds, she allowed herself to fall into this sensory world that soothed her into a state of relaxation she hadn't felt in months. Her breathing quickened. The air brushed her nose and then lips. Her mind spun with possibilities.

"That's why I love this moment. There're no sounds of nature in the night when you live in a cell," he whispered.

The way he said cell tugged at her heart, and she knew this man had suffered. And in that moment, she knew without a doubt. The Declan Mills who cut flowers, cooked dinner, and helped her nana eat could never and would never embezzle money for his own personal gain. "You're innocent, aren't you?"

He jerked and pulled away from her, but she grabbed hold of his forearms, staying his movement. "There's no way a man like you ever committed a crime. I don't care if you were convicted. You didn't do it." She swallowed the stump-sized lump in her throat. "Did you?"

He looked toward the twinkling stars, as if to find the right answer. "It doesn't matter." His hand grazed her cheek, and he looked at her with an intensity that made her squirm. "I am and always will be a convicted felon. Not a man worthy of a second thought from you. You deserve so much better. A life without complications and prejudice."

She smiled inside and out and let out a snicker.

"What?" he asked, taking a step back as if to analyze further.

"Have you noticed what I look like? Complications and prejudice, I've lived with my entire life. You'll have to do better than that to scare me away." She picked up her shears and returned to work, feeling like she'd won a battle for now, but based on his slouched posture and downcast gaze, he fought an internal war that would either tear him apart and make him run, or he'd surrender to the possibilities of a future. A future that could include her.

TEN

The dimly lit office only compounded the intimate feel of the room. Declan remained on the other side of the bench, organizing the flowers so that it would be easier for Felicia to design the arrangements.

All morning as they sat in silence, he made a mental bullet point of reasons they couldn't be together. Ex-con was at the top, but it was more than that. He'd never want to start a life with someone when he was poor and had no real future prospects. He didn't care that his boss was a woman. It was the fact that she *was* his boss for the only job he could find. A job that meant he would stay out of jail.

Each time her hand grazed his, he forgot all about the reasons.

"You're such a lifesaver." She glanced at her watch. "Will you ride with me into town? I need to see the girls, and we can grab some coffees and breakfast. I think we deserve it."

He ran his finger along the stem he'd dethorned before passing it to Felicia. "I can get to work on the front field, weeding and fertilizing."

"No way. You've been working for hours already. Besides,

there are rules about mandatory breaks and such. You wouldn't want to get me in trouble, would you?"

"No, of course not." He enjoyed her playful wink and nudge. A nudge to start facing life instead of hiding out in his camper. The way her voice sounded light and calming, he started to believe a life beyond prison was possible. "For the first time, I actually want to go into town. I'd like to start showing my face more and talking to people if I'm to continue working here. I don't want them seeing me as a strange hermit who hides on your property. Besides, I like the people of Sugar Maple, and as much as I shouldn't care, I'd like them to accept me."

"Then it's settled. Let's finish up the centerpiece, and then we'll head out." She arranged them, took them apart, and then rearranged them. The way she angled her chin and studied every side showed how much pride she took in her work. With nothing else for him to do to help her, he scanned the bookshelf.

"Do you mind?" He pointed to an agricultural manual.

"Help yourself."

He opened the book and glanced through the table of contents. There were chapters on everything from planting, to watering, to climate, and more. "Can I borrow this? I'd like to know more about the business. I mean, the planting side of things."

She glanced at her watch again, and that's when he noticed the sour look on her face. "You're going to be handling so much more if Lacey arrives late again today. I won't have a choice but to let her go. I can't keep paying her. I have my nana to take care of, and I've been gone too much lately. I'm not good with the accounting stuff. She usually handles all that, and I look over everything. I'm thinking there's a promotion in your future to office manager."

A sting rushed through him. "I can't."

She blinked at him. "What do you mean? You can't what?"

"I can't work on any accounting for you." He sat straight, his spine rigid and his hands fisted. "I'm sorry. I can do anything else you need, but you'll have to hire someone else for the books." He stood and paced the floor, realizing even this job wasn't right for him. He'd thought manual labor would be a perfect task for now, but this complicated things.

A soft touch to his back relaxed his shoulders but tightened his chest.

"You don't have to worry. I know you didn't embezzle money. There's no way you could've done that."

"You're too good and trusting. Not everyone in this world is like you. You don't know me well enough to judge my innocence. Besides, I've already explained it doesn't matter if I did or didn't commit the crime. The paper says I did. That paper will always haunt my life. If something goes missing somewhere, I'd be the first person they would look at."

She nudged him to face her. He turned and looked down into her soft complexion that reflected the golden light. "I would never accuse you. You can trust me."

"It doesn't matter what you think. I'd be the first person arrested. Don't you get it? Once a criminal, always a criminal."

"Calm down." She placed her palm to his chest. "Your heart is beating wildly. I won't push you into work you don't feel comfortable with. I get it. People judge before they ever know the truth. I know how that feels."

He wanted to cover her hand with his and tell her she couldn't possibly, but when he saw the honesty in her eyes, he knew there was more.

"I've been judged my entire life because I look different. It's as if I'm a walking piece of paper that everyone can read. I'm not really black because my skin is too pale. I'm not really white because my hair is too dark. I've been called every name in the book, judged and persecuted, questioned by police when I walked down the road in Nashville. I know it isn't the same, and I don't mean to belittle what you're saying. I'm actually trying to tell you that I understand, and that's why I'd never put you in a situation like that. I promise. I understand guilty before proven innocent. Remember my father?"

She dropped her hand to her side and rested her forehead to his chest. "I hate that you've been through so much. You know you can tell me the truth. You can tell me what happened and I'll believe you. Sometimes it only takes one person." Her voice cracked, so he tipped her chin up and saw tears in her eyes.

That's when he realized she'd just shared her own truth. The girl who always negotiated life with a smile and a helping hand had opened up to him. He'd never felt so special...and afraid.

Her watch buzzed, startling them both to a safe distance. "Well, looks like I'm hiring an accountant, or I'll figure out how to do the books."

He took a deep breath and swallowed his fear. "I'll help you. Not with the books, per se, but I can teach you how to do them for yourself."

"That would be amazing. I've been able to do basic checks and balances, but I never really learned how to do more. Lacey fell into my lap when I needed help with the nursery. You can say a lot about her now, but that girl was born a wiz at numbers. It wasn't until she hooked up with that boy, Jason, and my grandmother had her stroke that things went awry. Everything has been out of control since."

She swiped tears from her eyes. "Well, guess we better get these delivered so we can have time later for you to teach me about numbers and I can teach you about plants."

A throat cleared from the doorway, drawing both of them to Lacey with her arms crossed and a look narrowed in on Declan that told him he was in trouble. "I was on time, but you didn't tell me to meet you in your office. After the last five years, you're just going to toss me aside for this man because he's good looking? And you accused *me* of choosing my boyfriend over you and this job..." Lacey sauntered past a shocked Felicia and gave Declan the once-over. "He shouldn't be around the books anyway. He's a criminal." The way she looked at him spoke volumes beyond her words. She wouldn't tolerate him messing up her life, and she was coming after him.

ELEVEN

Felicia checked on Nana, who was sound asleep in her bed. Good. She'd try to make it back before she woke, but just in case, she left a note that she'd bring breakfast home. She headed outside, shaking her head she closed the front door and walked toward Declan, who was standing by her truck.

"What's wrong?" he asked.

She glanced up at him, noticing he'd already dressed and combed his hair, making him look more put together than earlier. Not that she minded his rushed-out-of-bed-in-boxers look. She felt heat rising up her neck, so she pushed the memory from her head and joined him. "Nothing. I hate leaving Nana alone all the time."

"I can stay with her if you wish."

Felicia checked her watch. "No, it's okay. The home nurse should be here soon. I only worry because she has always been a grossly independent woman, and having a nurse help her dress makes her mad. She's promised me she won't try to do it on her own anymore, though. That's how she fell and sprained her wrist and got a black eye six months ago."

He toed the ground. "You're an amazing person, Felicia Hughes."

She didn't know what provoked the compliment, but she savored it like one of Carissa's homemade cinnamon buns on a cold winter morning.

He brushed by her and headed for the front door.

"Where are you going?"

"To stay here with your nana. There's nothing more important than family, and you need to go be with your friends and work on Mayor Horton's wedding flowers."

"But you had your heart set on going into town." Felicia reached out for him, but he was just out of her reach—the way he'd been since arriving several weeks ago. She'd thought having him here would open a door between them, but he'd locked it shut.

"There'll be other opportunities."

"But you said you'd never be alone in the house. That you couldn't chance it."

He shrugged. "I guess you and your grandmother are worth the risk this one time." He winked and then strutted into the house, leaving Felicia reeling with more questions than answers about Declan.

Her watch beeped with the announcement she had to leave now if she was going to make the meeting, so she'd have to revisit crazy-Declan-town later. Thankful he'd already loaded the floral arrangements into the truck, she hopped in and took off. Relief that her grandmother wasn't alone flooded her. For the first time in weeks, she felt like she was catching up on work, while not leaving her nana alone. A solid-oak-sized weight lifted from her shoulders, and she found herself humming by the time she reached Maple Grounds.

She pulled into a space out front and caught a glimpse of Carissa leaving her Sugar and Soul Bakery, giving a good-bye kiss to Drew Lancaster. The man had major OCD but had learned to deal with the quirky goings-on of Sugar Maple, all in the name of love for Carissa. Felicia had been concerned about Carissa after what happened with her fiancé running off with her best friend Judas Jackie over a decade ago, but any man who would tar and southernize himself to prove his love was good enough for her friend. Drew had won her over when he rescued and took in a kitten. The other Fabulous Five were more difficult, but in the end, they all accepted him.

Hopefully, they'd accept Declan in town someday. Felicia smiled and opened the door to retrieve the box of bouquets. When she turned, she discovered that Carissa had met Jackie at the corner. Wow, that was progress after so many years of fiancé-stealing-stress had infiltrated their friendship. Now that Carissa had a new boyfriend, apparently all was forgiven. Well, almost all. Some wounds healed slower than others.

Stella marched up to the truck, already dressed for work at the garage in her overalls. Good thing Knox Brevard liked Stella the way she was, a mesmerizing grease monkey, despite the doubts Felicia had in the beginning. Who knew an internet sensation could enjoy small-town living with a girl who was never designed to be shown off to the world on his arm.

"Let me help you with that." Stella reached into the car to retrieve the centerpiece. "These are beautiful. I think this is some of your best work."

"I think that boyfriend of yours is rubbing off on you." Felicia used her hip to close the door once Stella moved out of the way.

She harrumphed. "Why does everyone keep saying that? All you people need a life or smack upside the head to mind your own business."

"Ah, there's the Sassy Stella we all know and love." Felicia hotfooted it to Maple Grounds before Stella could retaliate, but she didn't move fast enough.

"You still housing the ex-con?" Stella's words weren't said in a bitter or harsh tone, but they were justified. How could Felicia ever show her that Declan wasn't the man they all thought him to be?

Carissa and Jackie made it to the door in time to open it for Felicia to carry in the flowers. Mary-Beth rushed from behind the counter, abandoning whatever mixture she was concocting, and pointed to the corner table. "Those are beautiful. Ms. Horton's going to love them."

Felicia nodded but couldn't leave it at that. "She could've come by to see them instead of us all meeting here. Is she going to pass up any opportunity to force the Fabulous Five to work together? I mean, we're all friends again so we don't need these games."

"Are we?" Jackie raised a brow. "Friendly and friends are two different things."

Felicia swept in to stop the dead-end conversation before anyone crashed and burned. "We're all happy for Ms. Horton and working together. That's what matters. I'd say that's what the Fabulous Five has always been about."

"And our Negotiator Felicia is back," Jackie said with sarcasm.

Felicia set the box of bouquets down. "What do you mean?"

Carissa dove between them with her sweet smile. "She only means that you've been distracted lately. Usually, you're in the middle of any dispute in town, and well, you haven't been for weeks. Not since Declan arrived in Sugar Maple."

"What disputes?" Felicia looked between them.

Stella sat down and propped her work boots up on the table. Felicia wanted to tell her to move them so as not to upset Mary-Beth but held her tongue. "Knox had it out with Lori yesterday over creative differences. Melba and Ms. Gina argued outside the recreation center over their seats on the bus. And Davey...well..."

"What happened with Davey?" Felicia couldn't help but ask.

Jackie slid into the chair across from Stella, crossing her legs with her high-fashion heels. "That's the point. You don't know."

Carissa tugged Felicia down next to her in the two open seats between Stella and Jackie. "We're concerned because you've been away and not around town the last few days. Not to mention we heard you fired Lacey and put Declan in her place."

Felicia shot up a hand, done with this intervention. "First of all, Declan has nothing to do with this, except the fact that he saved me this morning from not getting these done for Ms. Horton." She saw the raised brows and open-mouthed shocks of her friends. "Lacey never showed at the event the other day, and then she showed up hours late for work the next day—even after she and I talked and I was quite firm about it—and then this morning I asked Declan to help with the books because I may have to let her go since she's been so unreliable since she hooked up with that boyfriend of hers."

"Since when does Felicia fire people?" Stella asked with an undertone of accusation.

"When she's tired of being used and she's tired of working double to cover for an employee who isn't working, but most of all she's just plain tired." Felicia hunched over, her glorious mood from this morning fading. All she wanted to do was return to the nursery and to Declan, who made her feel better than her own friends did.

Mary-Beth delivered a steaming beverage to her, the aroma of lavender wafting from the cup. It was a London Fog made only the way Mary-Beth knew how.

Felicia took a sip and allowed the warmth to sink all the way to her toes before she faced her friends again. "Listen, I know you're all only looking out for me, and I'm not trying to hurt anyone. I'm only trying to run a business while worrying about Nana being alone. And for the first morning in almost a year, I can sit here and not stress about her because Declan is with her. You guys have it all wrong. He's not the man you think he is."

Mary-Beth sat at the only empty seat, pushing her bracelets up her arm so they wouldn't clank against the table, and then twirled her earring. A tell sign that she was carefully choosing her next words. "Who's Declan to you?"

The words were like a priest asking for a confession after she'd committed an ultimate sin. "He's kind, compassionate, strong, easygoing, helpful, and protective. Early this morning when I remembered the floral arrangements, I ran outside to cut the flowers and get to work. When I kicked a metal can across the sidewalk, he was out of bed and outside before he even dressed."

"Really, what does that beast of a man sleep in?" Jackie brushed her vibrant auburn hair behind her shoulder and quirked a devious smile.

"That isn't important."

"Apparently it is, since your cheeks match Jackie's nail polish," Carissa said in a soft but teasing tone.

Jackie held up a fire-engine-red painted nail.

"He had clothes on, if that's what you're implying."

"What kind of clothes?" Stella asked, apparently deciding this friendship circle of torture could be interesting.

"Boxers."

"And?" Mary-Beth asked teasingly.

"And...and that's it. But only because he was rushing to protect me. That was the point of my story." Felicia hid behind her drink, trying to cool her skin while drinking a hot beverage. Like this conversation, it was a no-win scenario, so she decided to bulldoze over the winks, smiles, and hair flips of judgment. "Then he worked with me all morning to get these ready for Ms. Horton."

"You mean while in his underwear?" Jackie said in a rated-R way.

"No. He was dressed. Now stop."

"Oh no, we broke Felicia. She's not trying to make us all happy." Stella sat forward, taking Felicia's hand with a pouty lip and mock-sentiment.

Felicia wasn't getting anywhere with them. That was the problem with lifelong friends... They always knew which buttons to push and how to twist your words. "Okay, enough. Believe me or don't. But I don't think you know him well enough to judge him."

"We don't have to. The courts already did," Stella grumbled.

Okay, Felicia could give Stella her bitter words because the man had brought her father back to town, but the rest didn't have a reason to hate Declan. "Because no one's ever been falsely accused. Maybe perhaps for graffitiing?" She eyed Stella with the you-know-it's-true look. "Not to mention the fact my own father was arrested for being at the wrong color at the wrong place at the wrong time. He's innocent."

Stella rolled her eyes.

"I don't know how he was sent to jail or the circumstances surrounding his sentencing, but I know that the man who is at my house isn't a criminal. Do you really think I'd leave him alone with my grandmother if I thought that?"

"No," Carissa said, her eyes softening along with her speech. "Listen, I didn't realize how hard it's been for you. I should have—we all should have. We'll figure out a schedule to stop in to check on your grandmother daily. That way you can have a little relief in your day. You have real friends here who want to help. We've all been so caught up in the Knox Brevard show that we missed how badly you needed us. Well, we're here now, so you don't need anyone else to help."

"Yep, I can come over tonight after I close up the shop," Mary-Beth offered.

"I can cover tomorrow morning," Carissa said.

Stella let go of Felicia's hand and sat up straight. "Yep, I got the next day."

A foot connected with Jackie's shin, and she jumped. "Right, I'll take the next. See. All good. Now you can settle down and fire that man."

Forcing her emotions to remain calm, Felicia set the beverage down on the table, scooted her chair back, and stood. "I can see now this has nothing to do with friendly love, but this is a staged friendervention. Where's Ms. Horton?"

They all looked at each other with the we're-so-busted look. "She called Carissa last night and told her to post pone today. Something about a mayoral emergency."

"Well, thanks for adding more stress to my life. As for me being broken? Maybe I am, but if anyone broke me, it's my friends, not Declan Mills."

TWELVE

It was a pleasant morning with Nana, a woman who refused to allow Declan to call her anything else. In the middle of playing cards, he realized where Felicia had inherited her quiet strength from. Although, by the fourth game of Canasta—a game he'd never played before—he realized Nana differed in one way from Felicia. She was ruthless. He didn't mind, though. If only he could have a relationship like this with his mother.

"You playing or daydreaming about my granddaughter?"

He shot straight in his chair, causing the delicate backing to crack. "What? No... Why would you ask that?"

Nana shifted her cards around the makeshift stand he'd created with a butcher block and a rubber band so she could play with one hand. "Because you're smitten with her. It's written all over your face, so don't deny it to me." A slight bit of spittle escaped from the drooping side of her lip, so he dabbed it with the handkerchief. This time, she didn't pull away or look upset. They'd found a rhythm between them that worked.

He took a moment to choose his words carefully, shifting the fifteen cards in his hands. There would be no denying his attraction to Felicia, not to Nana. She'd call him out and then challenge him until he confessed, so he stayed with the truth. With a deep breath, he abandoned his cards and looked her straight in the eyes. "No need to worry. I'd never pursue your granddaughter. She deserves much better."

"Hogwash." She fisted her good hand and hit the table, causing a few cards to fall from the rubber band. "You think I'll be around forever? Heck, I've got one leg, one arm, and half a face already in the grave."

"Don't say that." Declan shifted, causing more cracking noises in the chair.

"Listen, son. I've lived my life. I'm good to go home to my good Lord. The only reason I'm sticking around is for Felicia. I've tried to find her a man, but she's too obsessed with caring for me to allow herself to date. This morning was the best and only date she's had in over a year."

"This morning wasn't a date," he quickly corrected her. "Work. We were working."

"By dim light, alone, snuggled together amongst beautiful flowers?" she said in a *narrator of a romance movie* kind of way. "Lacey likes to gossip."

"Work." He huffed. "We going to play or talk all day?"

She leaned back. "Talk. I'm old and crippled, so I get what I want."

"Ha, I see your MO now." He didn't lean back to match her posture, afraid the chair might snap in half.

"Listen here, young man. When I'm gone, Felicia will be alone. I can't rest until I know she has someone important in her life."

"You don't understand."

"That you brought Stella's father here, that you're an ex-con, that your own mother doesn't want you to visit her?"

Every muscle in his body stiffened. "How'd you—"

"Know?" She chuckled, sending a little saliva spray over the table. "You don't think I would've allowed you to stay here if I didn't check you out, did you? I might be old, but I'm a town elder. I know more than you could imagine. Like why your mother is upset with you."

"Hates me." He sighed, sending all the tension from his body, replaced by the weight of defeat.

"She suffers from dementia. She'll hate everyone. Trust me. I lost my best friend to the disease. In the end, she called me every name and accused me of stealing the man she loved away from her. Well, the last part had some truth, but we'd patched that up years ago."

He studied the soil in his nails, a sight that brought a feeling of accomplishment and hope to him. It represented an honest day's work, living in the outside world, by Felicia's side.

"Unless your mama hates you for another reason."

He didn't answer, knowing that lying wouldn't be an option, and the truth brought up way too much that he'd buried long ago.

"I see." She winked the side of the cloudy silver eye. "No need to explain. Just tell me one thing."

"What's that?"

"Do you regret it? Whatever your mother hates you for?"

He thought about it for a moment, but no other path would've kept his mother safe and well. "No. Not even for a second."

Nana drew two cards. "I win again."

He didn't have to look to know she had. The woman was a card shark. Good thing he wasn't a betting man. That was his father's trait, not his own. Too bad he'd bet all their lives and lost.

"Can I offer one more piece of advice?"

He smiled at Nana. "Do I have a choice?"

"Nope." She attempted a smile, but only one side lifted,

filling out her cheek, while the other one remained low and unresponsive. But he saw something in that smile, a beauty that must've turned men's heads in her day.

"Then shoot."

"Try opening up to Felicia. Trust her with your truth. Even if only a little of it."

He thought about her words for a moment. "But if I do that, it would mean that we were connecting on more than a boss-employee level."

"Would that be so bad?" Nana asked.

Her words were like the keys to his cell hanging just out of reach.

"Don't answer that." Nana pulled her cards free and stacked them with the others. "Shuffle and deal. I'm ready to beat you again."

Felicia's truck crunched gravel nearing the house.

"Later. I want to go help Felicia first. Stay right here. I'll be back in a few minutes." He catapulted out of his chair to the front door until he realized he'd showed too much eagerness under Nana's watchful eye. He turned to see her give an all-knowing nod, and for a minute he believed the woman did know everything. Things he didn't even know about himself.

He rushed to Felicia, excited to see her as if they'd been apart days instead of hours. She held out bags with logos to a place he'd never seen before. Certainly not a place from Sugar Maple. She looked dejected, the way she held out the food to him with little effort and her gaze traveled everywhere but at him. "What's wrong?"

She lifted her chin. "Nothing. I just thought it would be good to bring something different home to Nana. How was your morning with her?"

He decided to let it go. Whatever was bothering her wasn't

his business unless she wanted to share. "Good. She taught me how to play Canasta."

"Oh no." She lifted his free hand and studied his arms and then his face. "I don't see any bruises or cuts. You must've let her win."

"Let her? She's ruthless. I think she'd put any player to shame." The aroma of fries made his stomach growl. "Guess it's time for brunch."

"Guess so." She followed him inside, where Nana was making a not-so-fast escape. Cards were scattered on the floor and the chair was tipped over, but to his relief she was standing.

"Where you going in such a rush?" Felicia asked, tossing her purse onto the armchair and grabbing hold of Nana's bad side.

She swatted Felicia with her good hand. "Stop your fussing. I'm tired and going to my room. I'll eat later. Besides, I'm not crashing any dates."

"This isn't a date," Felicia said too quickly for Declan's taste. Despite all his protests about getting too close, somehow he'd already connected with her in a dangerous way. Dangerous to his heart and pride.

Nana shuffled toward the back hall with her cane, leaving an uncomfortable silence in the living room. He retrieved some plates but felt like something had to be said. "Date? Ha. If I were to take you out on a date, it wouldn't be fast food thrown on plates at your kitchen table."

She sauntered into the kitchen with a sway to her walk. "Really? Tell me, Mr. Declan Mills. What would you do if you took me on a date?"

"If it were a real date, I wouldn't take you to a five-star restaurant in town."

"That's good because we don't really have any. Well, we have a nice steak place outside of town." She shrugged and hopped up onto the kitchen counter, watching him retrieve four plates out of the cabinet as if he lived there. "Then where would you take me?"

"*If* this were a date, I'd spend all day creating the perfect homemade picnic lunch, and then I'd surprise you in the center field to watch the sunset." He placed two plates on the table, opened the bag, and set the breakfast sandwiches and potatoes on them. The smell of bacon and eggs filled the room, but it was only lukewarm since she'd obviously driven a good distance to get them. "I'd spread out a blanket, place candles in the center, and offer you my hand to sit." He tossed the bag into the trash and walked over to her at the counter, where he held out his hand.

"If this were a date." She winked and slid her fingers into his palm. "And then what?"

"And then I'd move in close so I could enjoy the aroma of your shampoo and the brush of your skin to mine."

Her lips parted and her eyes hooded. "And if it were a date. I wouldn't move away."

His skin heated at the sight of her full lips, long lashes that accentuated her bright eyes, and the faintest freckles on her cheeks. "If this were a date."

THIRTEEN

The next morning, Felicia awoke to the smell of fresh bacon and eggs. She rolled over and saw it was six thirty. When had she managed to fall asleep? All night her mind had swirled with the knowledge that Declan had opened his heart to her, if only for a few seconds. If only enough to provide a fleeting glimpse of his romantic side. A side she wanted to see more of in the future.

Felicia had never been the type to pursue a man, and if she thought for a second Declan wasn't interested, she'd shut her emotions down and move forward with her life. But the way he looked at her on their "non-date" made every part of her wake up from a yearlong slumber. The guy she'd been dating before Nana had her stroke had spent five minutes at the hospital and then taken off. He wasn't strong enough to handle a long-term obstacle in their relationship. She'd dodged that speeding train at the crossroads of Happily Ever After and Destined to be Abandoned.

Declan was different. He'd jumped right in to helping with her grandmother without even a pause. What kind of man did that? One who wanted to pull his weight, as he'd reminded her often. She shook her head, deciding that there was a glimmer of hope for her to learn more about him, but it would be a long road with many potholes.

The aroma drew her from bed, but she made a stop to freshen up and check herself in the mirror. She wasn't one for primping all the time, but she decided to dab on a little mascara and lipstick. Nothing too obvious but enough to make her look like she hadn't just rolled out of bed. Instead of pulling her hair back immediately, she decided to leave it down. Once a girl told her she had the most beautiful, unique midnight colored hair, and she'd spent too much time thinking it was her best feature over the years. Still, she left the bathroom feeling like she was a little more ready to face Declan.

He stood over the coffeepot, staring at it as if he were about to operate or murder the machine. It appeared as if he'd made his own effort to look nice this morning. Was that for her benefit?

"What's wrong?" She startled him, causing him to flinch.

"Oh, nothing. I can't figure out how to work the machine, or I didn't do something right."

"It's temperamental. Sometimes you have to give it a smack on the side. I know I need to replace it, but I haven't had the chance. Since I was the only one who drank coffee until you arrived, I didn't prioritize it."

"You never prioritize yourself, do you?" Declan didn't say it in an accusatory way, more with a hint of admiration. He tapped the side, as if the coffeemaker were made of glass.

She laughed. "You won't hurt it. Give it a good whack like this." With her hand splayed, she hit the side of the contraption. It gurgled and spit tar-colored goo. "Ugh. Guess I need to work on it."

She turned to face him and enjoyed the close proximity of

him leaning over her to see the coffeemaker. His gaze traveled down to her, and he took in a deep breath, filling his broad chest. Was it every woman or just her that enjoyed being close to a man with a strong frame? She was an independent woman yet liked to feel taken care of all at the same time. A walking contradiction, but a woman wanted what she wanted.

The dogs barked wildly outside, and lights warned of an approaching car. A few moments later, footsteps sounded from the front walkway.

Knock. Knock. Knock.

She had to keep from snarling at the intrusion. Who would choose this ungodly hour to show up at the house? Okay, that wasn't what made her miffed. Who interrupted a stolen private moment in her kitchen with Declan so close and relaxed?

He stiffened and looked to the door. "Wait here. I'll see who it is."

The man was like a watchdog protecting their home and property at all times.

"Relax. We live in Sugar Maple. Nothing exciting ever really happens around here."

He quirked a brow. "Like two ex-cons driving into town and one of them threatening Stella?"

"Point taken." She stayed back, allowing him room to see there wasn't evil at every bend in the road. Perhaps someday he'd relax and enjoy life. With her.

He opened the door to Stella and Carissa. It didn't even take twenty seconds for Stella to barge in with her sassiness. "Aren't you over here a little early for an employee, Mr. Mills?"

Felicia bolted into the living room with her own protective nature rearing into action. "He's welcome here anytime."

Stella passed a coffee to Felicia and one to Declan. "Sorry. Trying here." She took one of the two cups Carissa had and plopped down on the sofa. Apparently they were staying awhile.

Carissa sniffed the air. "Who's cooking? That smells amazing."

"Not Felicia, then," Stella teased.

"I am. I better get back to it. Thanks for the coffee." Declan retreated from the room like a large, handsome guppy fleeing from tiger sharks.

Carissa opened her arms, holding her coffee to the side. "Good morning. Sorry to intrude so early, but we wanted to apologize." Her arms wrapped tight around Felicia to let her know she missed her as much as Felicia had missed her friends. "We have no right to pass judgment. If you think Declan is a good man, then we should trust you."

"Yeah, what she said." Stella hid behind her coffee, and Felicia knew she had a lot to say but Carissa had convinced her to keep her mouth shut. That was asking too much, though. "Does he let himself in whenever he wants now?"

"No, I'm guessing Nana is up and let him in and then went back to bed. She only sleeps three or four hours at a time. He refuses to enter the house without permission and never alone." Felicia couldn't hide her disappointment at his distance, and she knew her friends saw her frustration without her admitting it aloud.

The sound of an egg cracking and sizzling in a frying pan told Felicia that Declan was working on preparing food for all of them, so she gestured for Carissa to sit in Nana's chair and Felicia took her place on the other side of the coffee table in the rocker. "You came out here at this hour to say you're going to try to accept Declan? It could've waited, or you could've called."

"Told you she'd see through us." Stella sat forward, resting her cup on the tabletop. "We trust you and all, but we also know you're a little blind when it comes to him. I get it. Knox turns me around and convinces me to do things like star in his internet show and stuff. No one but him could get me to do that. Some men have power over us, and no matter what we do we don't see their flaws until it's too late. Of course, Knox's flaws are ones I can live with. Can you live with Declan's? Do you even see them yet?"

"Yes, I'm not blind. We all have faults." Felicia glanced over her shoulder to make sure Declan was still cooking, and she lowered her voice. "The man has a mega wall up between us, so you don't have to worry. He's not letting me near him. Beyond that, he's the best man I've ever met. He's kind, considerate, compassionate. He's helped with my nana. Look, he's cooking breakfast for you now, even though you were rude when you arrived." She tried to tone down her irritation, but her rushed speech and low tone got away from her.

"An act," Stella grumbled. "I mean, it could be. You see that, right?"

"Of course, but I don't think so. I'm not sixteen, and I'm not easily manipulated. Yes, I wanted to give him a chance and that's why he's here, but now I've gotten to know him better and it's not about that anymore." Felicia inhaled a deep breath to calm her emotions. Since when did she get so riled up when talking to Stella? "I know you haven't forgiven him for bringing your father to Sugar Maple. What would it take for you to feel more comfortable with him here?"

"Ah, there's our negotiator." Carissa smiled.

They both looked to Stella. She shrugged. "Knox asked me the same question yesterday. He told me if I face what was bothering me, I'd feel better and avoid strain on an important relationship in my life."

"Smart man," Carissa said.

Stella smiled in a way she'd adopted since Knox arrived into her life. A real smile with true happiness behind it. "I guess knowing why he did it would help."

"Then I'll try to explain."

They all startled at Declan's deep voice entering the room. He handed a plate to Felicia with an apprehensive look on his face. She wanted to save him from the Stella inquisition, but she couldn't. When Stella wanted an answer to something, she wouldn't stop until she found it.

Once Declan handed Carissa her plate, she balanced it on her lap, and he put Stella's on the coffee table in front of her. No one touched their food, though. Instead, they all looked up at Declan, who shifted between feet with his hands clutched in front of him.

After he closed his eyes and reopened them, he said, "Your father begged me to bring him to Sugar Maple one day. He told me of how his daughter was mixed up with some YouTuber sensation that was going to ruin her reputation and life. It took some convincing, but I agreed to bring him here."

"My father is more of a bully than a politician. I don't buy it." Stella's words were harsh. Too harsh.

"You asked for an explanation, and he gave you one." Felicia fought to control her voice to keep it steady the way she did when she was trying to make peace between people in an argument, but she couldn't remain neutral. For once, she'd chosen a side against one of her friends.

"No, she's right. That was the validation for my actions but not the reason for my decision." Declan lowered his head and studied his hands. A great shame etched in the lines around his eyes.

They all sat quietly for a moment, waiting for him to continue. Carissa with soft eyes and Stella with a jackhammer gaze, as if she were ready to beat the truth out of him.

"When I was released from jail, I discovered your father was manipulating my mother." Declan's voice dipped into pure pain. "My mother suffers from dementia. At the time, it was early stages, but she was easily manipulated out of her life savings."

Stella's expression changed from hatred to the familial that's-my-father wilting of her brow. "You couldn't tell your mother what was going on and kick my father out of her life?"

"Not when your mother has a restraining order against you."

Carissa gasped. Felicia stiffened in the chair, but as with everything about Declan, she knew there was more behind that story. "Why did she file a restraining order? How did she file it if she has dementia?" she asked intently.

Declan ran a hand through his hair, disheveling it from its perfectly gelled appearance.

"It does sound like there's more to this story." Carissa looked to Felicia to let her know she'd listen before passing judgement. "Please, Stella and I promise not to share it beyond this room. We're not part of the Sugar Maple gossip line."

He rubbed his forehead, as if to dislodge a memory he didn't want to see. "She didn't actually file it. Your father did. Well, he had her sign the paperwork, but my mother has hated me for several years now. It wouldn't have been too hard for him to convince her."

Felicia rose from the chair, blocking his view from the others, and took his cheeks between her hands. "I don't believe your mother hated you. This is another case of you pushing people away. Tell me the truth. Why do you think your mother hated you?"

His gaze locked with hers, his body stiff and distant. "My dad died because I was sent to jail for embezzling money from his company." As if his shield snapped back into place, his gaze darkened. "As I told you before, I'm an ex-con and I work here. That should be all this is, and I won't be a problem that drives conflict between you and your friends." He took a step back, as if to break their connection, and looked to Stella. "If you're not satisfied by my explanation and if you want me to leave, I will respect that. Let me know what you decide. I'd never want to bring pain or drama into Felicia's life." And with that announcement, he strode out the front door.

FOURTEEN

Declan threw two bags of organic mulch over his shoulder and marched to the outer field and then repeated the act four more times. By the fifth trip, he was drenched in sweat, so he took a quick glance at the house. With no sign of the girls, he went to the hose, pulled his shirt off, and doused himself with water. It drenched him from head to toe, but he didn't care. Refreshing, cooling, and energizing was what he needed at the moment. Then back to work he went.

There was something about manual labor that made him feel worthy. He'd never felt so fulfilled when he was working at the large firm on the Upper East Side before he moved home to help his father. Women coveted him. His boss relied on him. He was important yet felt empty all those years. Now, at almost thirty, he could hold his head higher than he did when he was an important person to many people. That was the problem during that time in his life... He had many people who wanted to be around him—heck, many people who wanted to *be* him— but that left a person lonely. Even his relationships were fleeting. With each step he climbed to the next rung of the proverbial corporate ladder, he'd leave a girl behind. Now, he wanted nothing more than to stay put on solid ground. But could he? His future rested in the hands of the people of Sugar Maple, specifically the Fabulous Five.

He mopped his brow with his shirt and then opened the mulch and spread it around the newly planted shrubs. The compost of animal manure and coarse material made for a perfect nutrient-rich compound with less salt. He'd read about this in the book he'd borrowed from the office. With care, he spread the material around each of the plants, careful not to touch the trunk, not to layer so high that it would choke the roots but enough to protect the roots from heat and rot.

The sound of car doors closing told him that the girls were leaving. It had taken an hour or two for them to deliberate. Was that good or bad for a friends-decides-a-man's-fate kind of trial? He decided to keep his mind on his work since there was nothing he could do to change anyone's mind. He'd learned a long time ago to state the facts and walk away because arguing just makes you look guilty.

He sat on the ground, eyeing the field and enjoying the peace it provided.

"Wow, you've done a lot. And the way you spread the mulch is perfect. How did you know?"

"Book." One word. That's all he could manage if he didn't want to lose his temper, demanding to know if the verdict was in. How had one little job become so important to him? Yes, he needed it so that he could pay restitution, but it had become more than that in a short time. He'd enjoyed the physical aspect of the work, watching the plants he'd fertilized bloom, and the company he'd kept. After living within gray walls, in gray cells, in gray uniforms, the colors were like medicine to his cancerous soul.

"Can I ask you a question?" Her voice sounded delicate, as if she feared he'd bolt if she spoke with too much authority.

"You're the boss."

"Why did you say that your mother hated you? I don't believe you." She settled by his side, resting her hand on his thigh. "You're always trying to push everyone away, even when you want things to work out. At least, I think you want to stay here. Sometimes I can't tell."

"I do." He looked at her face only inches from his own. Captivating was the word that popped into his head. More so than the flowers or the trees or the sunshine.

"Then tell me, why do you keep pushing me away, trying to drive a wedge between us and force me to send you away?" Her mouth quivered with a slight vibration. Did she care that much?

He tore his gaze from hers, unable to face the fact he'd ever cause her the most minuscule of discomforts, but she needed to know. He'd slipped and allowed himself to believe there could be something between them. He moved to a sack to empty it over the next section of plants. "It's true. She hated me because I was convicted of embezzling the money from my father's company and caused him to have a heart attack and die. The stress was too much for him."

For the longest of moments, he waited for her argument. Once he'd dumbed the bag and spread the organic bits around the trunks of the thriving plants, he stood, clapped his hands to free them of the remnants, and forced himself to face her. He didn't have to look far. She was there. Next to him, mouth ajar and the sweetest of expressions on her face.

"I understand now. I can't believe it took me so long to figure this out, but I know."

He stiffened. "You know what?"

"That it wasn't you. I mean, I always knew you didn't commit the crime, but I couldn't figure out why you took the fall. Now I know."

"What? No, you couldn't know. How?" he stammered.

She touched his face with her fingers, tracing along his jawline and then down to his chin. He couldn't breathe beyond the confusion of her words and her closeness. Two years was a long time for a man to be away from women. And almost thirty years was too long to be far from Felicia. Her eyes softened and she bit her pink lip, as if she feared her words were true or, worse, false. "You went to jail to protect your parents."

He sucked in a quick breath.

"I'm right. I know I'm right." She clutched both his cheeks between her palms, her gaze trapping his. "Your father. Yes, you did it to protect your father. I haven't figured out why, but I know I'm right."

"How do you know?"

She stood on her toes and pressed her lips to his ear. "Because I know you're a good man. You're the best man I've ever met."

And with those words, she turned him inside out and backwards, offering him possibilities. Possibilities he hadn't dared believe in until now.

The possibility of Felicia in his life.

FIFTEEN

The noises in the garden faded into a blur. Felicia brushed her lips along Declan's salty cheek, slid along his jawline, and hovered near his lips. The overwhelming desire to kiss this vulnerable, strong, sensitive, selfless man took hold, so she brushed the corner of his mouth.

He lurched back and held her at arm's length. "Wait. It doesn't matter. None of it matters if I put a rift between you and your friends. I won't be the cause of ruining your life. There are too many women who already hate me in this world."

"Stay."

"What? Is that what Stella and Carissa said? Did they agree that I wouldn't ruin your life?"

"Do you care for me?"

He shook his head, but not as if saying no, more in confusion. "What?"

"It's a simple question. Answer it."

"Yes, but that doesn't matter."

"It matters more to me than if my friends approve," she said with an air of frustration.

"It's a problem if your friends have an issue with me." He laced his fingers behind his head and looked toward the sky.

"Why?" She lowered to her feet flat on the grass.

He closed the distance this time. "Because your happiness means more than any job to me."

She blinked, processing his words but wanting more. "Why?"

"I want you to be happy, and I don't want to bring any more trouble to you. You've been more than kind to a stranger. You've given me a place to put my camper, allowed me into your home."

"You're no longer a stranger. I know you." She longed to make him see how much of a gift he was to her.

"Aren't I? I mean, you haven't known me long, yet I've put a rift between you and your friends."

"I see." She took a step back. "If that's all you care about, then yes, you can stay. You've got the stamp of approval from Stella and Carissa." She about-faced and headed to the office.

"Wait, what's wrong?" he asked, following two steps behind her through the cobblestone walkway to the office.

"Nothing. We're good. I'm your boss, you can stay, and all is right."

"It doesn't sound right."

He remained in the doorway while she went inside to shift papers around and grumble about how Lacey hadn't shown yet today. He had to see how much better he made things around here.

"I have one more question," he asked in a deep tone.

She dropped the papers and huffed. "What's that?"

"Do you want me here?"

His words sat in the air along with the dust and pollen and fear. "If that's what you want, then yes."

He took one step that took him to the center of the room.

His bare chest radiated heat, or was that her heart? "That's not what I asked."

His chin rose, his muscles tightened.

"Yes," she whispered. "I want you to stay."

"Then I'll stay," he said with a broad smile that reached his eyes.

"Great. Glad that's settled."

"Not quite."

She arched a brow. "What else is there to discuss?"

"This." He closed the distance between them and took hold of her face, guiding her onto her toes as he arched down over her. His lips pressed to hers. Her body erupted into a series of heartwarming palpitations from her toes to her chest. Her knees shook, and her mind trembled with thoughts of happily ever after. She'd never felt so treasured, worshiped, alive.

It was a sweet, I-cherish-you kind of kiss, yet it awakened her in a way no other man had.

He moved his lips away, but his hands remained firm and his forehead rested to hers.

She couldn't open her eyes, fearing he'd run if she did. And she didn't want him to ever run from her again.

"I know I'm being selfish, that you deserve so much better than me."

"No." She opened her eyes and grabbed his shirt so he couldn't run.

He smiled and his thumb grazed her lips, distracting her from any further words. "But...but when you pulled away, I didn't like it. As if one cross word from you would destroy me. No woman has ever had such power over me before. I've never met a woman, any person, with so much heart and bravery. Those school kids who once teased you were right about one thing. You're one of a kind. You're the most giving, caring, strongest person I know." His breath caressed her lips with the promise of another kiss. "You're uniquely beautiful. God made you special, and you should own that."

"I knew you were trying to force me out."

Lacey's words shattered the most perfect moment in Felicia's life. She wanted to scold Lacey for her intrusion, especially since she was due at work hours ago.

Felicia hadn't heard a car or dogs barking. She'd been lost in all that was Declan Mills. Apparently, he had been too, the way he jumped too far from Felicia. When he bolted from her side, the evidence of why Lacey had been late was etched in dark purple and red crusted blood around her right eye and lips.

Felicia went to Lacey's side, despite her desire to remain with Declan, who faded into the shadows. "What happened? Were you in an accident?"

"No. You did this!" Lacey's words were bitter and wounded.

Declan moved into the light, his gaze animalistic. "Who did this to you?"

"Who?" Felicia looked closer and could see the yellowish outline of knuckles on her cheek.

"You did. I yelled at Jason that I needed this job." Tears fell from Lacey's eyes, streaming down her face.

"He did this?" Felicia asked, still unable to comprehend the markings a man put on her face.

"It's your fault. You told me I'd be fired if I wasn't here at seven in the morning. Jason doesn't get up until eight. I knew this, but I pushed for you."

Lacey crumpled in front of them. Declan caught her before her knees hit the ground and settled her into the desk chair. When he stood to the side, Felicia saw something in Declan she didn't think was possible—a look of pure hate. He snagged the keys from the hook with a murderous expression narrowed at the door and his feet already moving. "I need to borrow the truck."

Felicia was caught between holding Lacey up in the chair and charging after Declan. "Wait, you can't. You're on probation. Let the police handle this." Her words fell somewhere between the doorway and Declan's ears, because she heard the truck rev to life and spin on the gravel. If he was fast enough, he'd catch him on the one road out of town. In that moment, she knew her hopes and dreams were being crushed under those tires.

Felicia slid her phone from her pocket and called Stella. The one girl who might understand this situation.

"Hey, you already decide to dump the guy?"

"He's going after Jason."

"What?"

"Lacey's boyfriend. She showed up here beaten and bruised by her boyfriend, and something in Declan snapped. I don't know what to do. The way he looked, I can't explain it, but it scared me."

"Hold on a second." Stella covered her phone and mumbled something for a few seconds before returning. "I'm on it. Don't worry. You stay with Lacey."

"I know you don't like Declan. You think he's not good enough for me, but please, promise me you'll stop him from doing anything stupid."

"I like Declan fine. As for who is good enough for you? No one. If this is the man you care about, I'll help. Don't worry. I've got this." The phone went dead, and if Felicia didn't know better, the fact that Declan had run off half-cocked was something Stella could respect. And if anyone knew how to handle a temper, it was Stella.

Lacey finally stopped sobbing enough for Felicia to get her out of the chair and take her inside the house, where Nana stood at the window with her cane. "What's going on?"

She pursed her lips at the sight of Lacey. "Oh, you poor

dear. Come sit." She scooted out of the way of the couch and plopped down, patting the seat next to her. "Tell Nana everything. I'm here now." She took Lacey into her arms and held her the way only grandmothers could. "You go after Declan," she told Felicia. "I've got Lacey. She and I need to have a conversation about life choices. I've got a story to share with her that might help."

"I don't have a car." Felicia looked to the window. "Declan took my truck."

"You've got friends, don't you?"

"Right." She slid her phone out of her pocket and texted Carissa. *I need a ride to town ASAP. Please help.*

She didn't have to even wait for a response. Three dots danced instantly.

Drew is on his way. Stella filled us in.

Felicia looked at Nana and Lacey and felt led to say one more thing before leaving, so she knelt in front of them and rubbed Lacey's back. "Listen, I didn't know how bad things were with Jason, but I should have. I miss the girl I once knew before he came into your life."

"Miss me? You've been too busy for me," she said in a bitter tone.

Felicia knew her words came from pain and embarrassment. She was only lashing out because the man she thought she loved betrayed her. Something no woman ever wanted to face.

"I'm here now."

"No, you're running off again, after him. You care more about an ex-con than me. I thought we were like sisters."

And with that, Felicia realized she could be compassionate but also firm. She stood and looked down at Lacey from a motherly, authoritative angle. "Then, as your big sister, I'm going to give it to you straight. Your choice to be with that man is what is driving a wedge between you and everyone else. I love you like a sister, that's true. And that's why I'm not going to tolerate you being abused by the man. That's why I'm leaving. Not only to go after Declan but to make sure that Jason stays far away from you."

"No, wait. That isn't fair. He loves me, and he said he was sorry. He doesn't do well when he's woken up early, especially after a night out drinking with the boys."

Felicia looked to her grandmother, who nodded. "Don't worry. I'll start some reprogramming while you're away. I know exactly how she feels. My first husband was a man who chose to communicate with his fists."

Felicia blinked at her, opened her mouth and then shut it again.

"We all have regrets in our past," Nana said with an undertone of deeper meaning. "But this is a story for another day. Right now, I think your ride is here. Go get Declan and bring him home." Nana waved her bad arm a little higher than she normally did.

Declan had been good for her. She'd been getting herself up and feeding herself since his arrival. That man was something special, and she wasn't about to lose him, but at the same time, looking down at Lacey made her second-guess Declan and the way he took off. Was he, too, a man prone to violence after living in prison for two years? That had to change a man, even the best of men.

Even Declan.

SIXTEEN

A sign flashed fifty-two miles. Underneath it read speed limit thirty-five. Declan moved his foot to the brake, forced to obey the speed limit if he didn't want a ticket. A ticket that could send him to jail while on probation. The one good thing about the law of speed meant a man had time to cool off.

What had happened to him? Since when did he erupt like that? The sight of the young girl stirred something in him. The idea of any man causing such pain, especially someone close to Felicia, broke him.

When he pulled into the town square, the flowers Felicia had planted in the center calmed his anger to a simmer, but Jason still had to be dealt with. The image of the younger man's fist print on Lacey's face gutted him. He pushed on the gas and turned right onto the street heading toward Riverbend, sure he'd catch Jason on the on the way or once he arrived.

Stella and Knox stood in the center of the road holding up their hands, as if they could stop a half-ton truck with their bodies. He hit the brake, squealing to a stop, and hopped out. "What're you doing? I could've hit you!"

"What are *you* doing?" Stella marched at him, but Knox

took hold of her arm. "You're freaking Felicia out. And right after I gave my stamp of approval for you."

"I'm not going to harm the guy."

"Really?" Stella asked in a more thickened accent than normal. "So, you're not running off full of hate? You've thought this through, and you're just going to have a friendly chat with the man?"

He cleared his throat and lifted his chin. "Right. A firm chat."

"Then you might want to put on a shirt." Knox pointed at his bare chest.

Declan had been so riled up that he didn't even realize he'd run off without getting dressed first. It was as if he was back in jail. He'd changed over those years into a man he didn't recognize at times. This was one of those moments. He'd always been put together, calm, sane.

He leaned against the side of the truck and ran his hands through his sweaty hair, realizing he probably smelled as bad as he looked. "I didn't mean to scare Felicia, but you should see that young girl with bruises and cuts."

Knox released Stella and slapped him on the shoulder. "I have no doubt any man would've done the same."

"But you're *not* any man. You're a man with a record," Stella said with no soothing adjectives or smiles. "That's the fact. Whether you did or didn't commit the crime, you're at the mercy of the courts, and I personally don't want my best friend pining over some man in prison because he committed assault while on probation, so get your act together."

"I thought I had." He shook his head and eyed the soil stuck to his stomach and shorts. "Something inside me clicked the second I saw her, and it was like a battle call. You were right all along Stella. Felicia shouldn't be with me. I'm a man still fighting his way through life as if I'm still in prison."

"I think you're being too hard on yourself," Knox said. "Most men would've felt the same way. Trust me, Drew and I both want to go visit this guy, and we didn't even see Lacey. As a matter of fact, maybe the three of us can go pay him a social call, but first, let's find out if she's willing to press charges. If she is, we'll let the police handle it and we'll help her get a restraining order. If not, then we'll pay him a visit. Deal?" He held out his hand, as if Declan was worthy of his approval.

He shook on Knox's plan and felt a hint of relief at the fact he didn't have to go to jail to help someone. A car pulled up behind them. "Guess I better move."

When he turned around, Felicia ran to him and threw her arms around his waist. "I was so worried." A second later, she stood back and smacked him on the chest. "What were you thinking?"

She was adorable when she scolded him. "I was thinking Lacey needed protection."

"Leave that to the police. You don't have to save her. This town will protect her. She's not on her own."

Declan shook his head. "I can't comprehend that. When Stella's father, Zach, hit my mother, the police did nothing, neighbors did nothing, and I did nothing." He bowed his head in shame. "He looked at me and told me he owned my mother and there was nothing I could do about it. I'd just been released from jail, and I didn't do what needed to be done out of fear of returning. I allowed that man to harm my own mother."

"No, you didn't. You got him away from her." Stella's words shocked him. "You did what you could to protect your mother. I see that now. I don't have to like it, but I can see it."

Felicia held tight to him. "You're not alone now."

He felt the love pouring from her. The way she looked at him told him she believed him to be a man of honor. A man who could give her the world. But how could he, when he couldn't even afford to give her flowers? "I appreciate the sentiment, but I'm not a member of this town and I never will be." He took a step away from her. "Stella and Carissa and the rest of your friends were right to be leery of me. I can't bring you what you want or what you deserve. I need to leave before you end up as heartbroken as Lacey is now." Without another word or another glance in fear he'd collapse before he even made it to the truck, he slid into the driver's seat.

Before he could put the truck in gear, Felicia hopped into the passenger side. "Nope. You're not leaving. Not now." She put on her seat belt and sat forward. "You promised to help me, and I'm holding you to that. This is my busiest time of year. You want to shut me out romantically, fine, but you're not leaving. You need the job as much as I need your help."

He gripped the steering wheel and willed himself to argue. "You have Lacey now. I assume she'll be on time now that it's over with that boy."

"Can she lift two bags of mulch at a time? Can she clear a field in a half a day? Can she make me smile?"

He cringed at her last words. "I'm not the right man for you. I know you don't like me saying I'm an ex-con, but now I know exactly what that means beyond the constant fear of being sent back. I changed during my time of incarceration. It hardened me in a way I can't let go."

She didn't touch him or use her feminine ways on him. She simply sat back and waited for him to drive. By the time they reached the square again, he'd already waffled on his intensions, but he knew he couldn't keep himself in check, not when he'd grown so fond of Felicia. He needed to leave, and he needed to leave now.

"By the way, your probation officer called, and I confirmed your employment. He says that's a step in the right direction, and if you hold this job and make restitution, you'll be able to remain a free man. If you lose this job and you can't find another one, you'll return to jail."

His mouth went dry. How could he leave if that meant returning to a cell? Yet, how could he stay if he was all worked up over Felicia and doing dumb things that would land him in jail? And there was Lacey... She was dangerous. A girl caught between infatuation and family could have devastating effects. The closer he got to Felicia, the more that girl would lash out at him in ways he couldn't even imagine. She'd already threatened to send him to jail. "I can't be with you."

She didn't argue, she didn't cry or protest, she only clasped her hands in her lap and said, "That's fine. We'll be boss and employee. And as my first order as your boss, you need to get us back to the house and finish that mulch by the end of the day."

The coldness in her voice disturbed him, but it's what he needed. A clear boundary between them. His probation officer had been right. He had one mission in life, to follow the steps outlined in his parole. Still, when he went to see him tomorrow, he'd ask again if he knew of any other jobs he could take. It would be best for everyone, but for now, he'd return to the field and work through his wants and desires to protect Felicia from a life she didn't deserve.

SEVENTEEN

The afternoon rolled into evening, and Lacey had finally calmed. Nana looked tired, and Felicia worried she'd taken on too much for one day. "Lacey, you're welcome to stay here tonight in the guest room. I know you're eighteen, but I still want you to call your mother and tell her you'll be here."

Lacey nodded, rose from the couch, and went to the guest room without a word.

Felicia took the opportunity to sit by her grandmother. "I think you should go rest. I'll call you when dinner's ready."

"You're not going to grill me about my first marriage? I mean, I thought you for one would demand to know why I never told you." Nana scooted sideways to face Felicia. "I know you don't like secrets."

Felicia let out a quick exhale. "It's fine. You don't have to tell me. That's your secret to keep. I'm only glad you were here to provide comfort to Lacey."

"I'm afraid that, despite my words, she's not going to agree to press charges."

Felicia felt a lightning bolt of anger flash through her.

Nana's hand slid over hers. "Now, child. You've never been

in this kind of situation, so don't judge. Jason has manipulated Lacey into believing she can't live without him. He's destroyed her self-esteem, made sure he alienated her friends and family. Trust me, I know the type. Although I've never spoken about my first husband, he gave me one gift. He taught me how to believe in myself and that I could manage life no matter what. And I didn't need anyone's help."

"Is that why you're so stubborn?" Felicia teased, not wanting to think about any man harming her grandmother.

"Yes, and that's why I've raised you to be independent. I never wanted an older man to sweep into your life when you were a teenager and convince you he was everything. Sometimes, I think I did too good of a job." She tightened her grip on Felicia. "Tell me, how did things go with Declan?"

Felicia collapsed back into the couch. "It didn't. One minute he's kissing me. The next he's pushing me away."

"Kissing?" Nana said in a suggestive tone. "Now I'm intrigued."

"Relax. Apparently, it meant nothing to him. All he cares about is remaining strong, independent, and free. Don't get me wrong. I understand. That's why I'm giving him space. He needs to figure out his own life before he can invite anyone in. I'm not sure why I fell so hard so quickly."

"Because he's the first man to ever turn your head and intrigue you. He's your equal when it comes to caring for others. A man who sees the world like you, despite the harshness he's witnessed." Nana smiled in her I-know-you-better-than-anyone kind of way. "Most boys you dated would bend over backwards to win you over with things that didn't have any meaning. They'd buy stuff like flowers, despite the fact you grew your own, but they were never really there for you. This man has done nothing but work to earn your respect. He might be poor financially, but he's rich in heart. He's demonstrated this by not only being the best worker you've ever known but also doing random acts of kindness—like cooking, even though he doesn't have to. I thank God every day for that." She winked.

Felicia eyed the kitchen and then the clock. If Declan followed his same pattern today as the other days, he'd be in here to cook dinner in about five minutes, and that caused her pulse to quicken. "He said he's doing that to earn room and board until he can afford his own food and to help pay electricity."

Knock. Knock. Knock.

Nana nodded toward the door. "By the expression on your face, you're hoping that's someone special." She leaned forward and hollered, her voice cracking from the strain. "Come in. Door's unlocked."

Declan stepped inside with something in his hands. "I hope I'm not too early, but I have something for Nana." He held out a rectangular object wrapped in brown paper.

As if a child at a fourth birthday party, she ripped through the paper. "What is it?"

"I made a functional stand for you to play cards. This way that pesky rubber band won't break, and the cards won't fall out and scatter all over the floor."

Were those tears in Nana's eyes? Felicia looked between her grandmother and Declan—a bond had formed in such a short time. He'd managed to crack the surface of the most stubborn woman in town, getting her to play cards and eat with him in the room. That man had done more than she or any therapist had been able to accomplish.

"Thank you, son. It's beautiful. I'll catch you after dinner for a game of Canasta. I'm feeling lucky tonight." She set the wood slat with ten clamps on the table and then pushed to stand. Declan had her cane at her side before Felicia could move.

Nana grabbed hold of the cane but looked back over her shoulder at Felicia. "Random acts of kindness. I rest my case."

In that moment, Felicia knew Declan was wrong about himself. Prison hadn't hardened him. He was as soft inside as Fluffy's fur. Now she just had to prove that to him.

Declan escorted Nana to her room and then marched to the kitchen without a glance at Felicia. His determination to avoid her cut her to the core, but she understood why and needed to keep her emotions out of this if she spoke to him.

Pans clanked and the stovetop clicked and then poofed with its flame.

A twitter in her chest made her take another second before she approached to calm her anxiousness. She took two long breaths and then plastered on a nonchalant expression and relaxed shoulders before strutting into the kitchen. "Can I help with anything?"

"No, I'm good, but thanks." Declan took chicken out of the refrigerator and sliced it into chunks.

"That was so nice of you to make that for Nana. It's amazing to see how much she's improved since you arrived." Felicia casually stepped over to the counter by the refrigerator and hopped up so she would be in his path whenever he had to get something. "The therapists had all given up, releasing her from care until she was ready to work harder. They said her insurance wouldn't cover any more since she'd plateaued."

"She's the one who wanted to play cards. I didn't do anything," he said in a defensive tone.

She closed her eyes and kept her cool, despite the fact she wanted to smack him in the back of the head. "Still, no one else could get her to even do anything. Do you know she talked about inviting people over to play cards? Maybe even taking a trip into town? That's huge. That's what you did."

He about-faced on her with a tight jaw, but his eyes softened the minute he focused on her. "Stop."

She raised her brows at him in an I-haven't-got-a-clue-what-you're-talking-about way. "What?"

His gaze traveled the length of her and then back to her face before he ripped his attention away and settled on the food he was sautéing in the pan. "You know what. We agreed that we would keep things platonic between us if I were to stay."

"This is a platonic conversation. You're the one who looks at me like you want more." She hopped down from the counter and headed for the living room, realizing one conversation wouldn't change things between them and she didn't want to make him run.

He turned, only a few inches from her, spatula in hand over the pan but his body toward her. "I'm sorry. You're right." He lifted his chin and took a breath that expanded his chest so far she couldn't help but remember what he'd looked like earlier today shirtless.

She concentrated on keeping her attention at chin height and above. Nana was wrong. It wasn't just about his heart. She'd never been attracted to a man physically like this before. Yes, she'd found men handsome, but this man, the man standing a foot away, was more primal, more intriguing than anyone she'd ever met. "Apology accepted. Can I set the table at least?"

He looked at her as if he'd found the gateway to heaven but he couldn't reach it. "Sure, thanks," he said in a hoarse, I-desire-you tone.

She ripped herself away from a budding moment, knowing she had to keep things steady and smooth for now. Any indication that they couldn't work together, she realized, would send him packing, and she couldn't have him sacrifice his entire future because she couldn't control her own romantic intentions. She'd never been so interested in a guy who wasn't reciprocating the affection, but she knew he cared. He fought it, but he did. She had to cling to that.

With a determination to remain cordial and light, she set the table and concentrated on the aroma of the food he was making. Pepper, garlic... What was that other scent? She closed her eyes and inhaled deeply, savoring the smell of...of...Declan.

Her eyes shot open, and she saw him standing near her with a large plate of chicken in his hands. "The rice should be done in a minute."

The door creaked open, and she'd never been so thankful to have an interruption when Declan was close.

Lacey entered the living room but stopped at the sight of Declan. "What is *he* doing here?"

The room filled with prickly thorns, and she thought she'd end up bloodied and cut if she stood between them for too long. She took a deep breath and forced a calmness she didn't feel. "Lacey, I love you. I want you to stay here for a while. You'll work and live here until you're back on your feet."

"Really?" Lacey threw her arms around Felicia, but Felicia nudged her a step away so she could finish. "I realize that you don't care for Declan, and I can't force you to see him as anything different than a threat to you—"

"I'm not threatened." She shot her chin so high, Felicia swore the girl's neck would crack.

"If you're to take me up on my offer, you will be kind and keep the peace. I will not have anyone feel unwanted in my home. Do you understand?"

Lacey nodded, but it wouldn't take even an hour before Felicia regretted her offer. By the time dinner was over, she was tired of the snide remarks. By the time the week was over, she was done with the rude comments. At the end of two weeks, she'd had enough and swore she'd put a stop to the spoiled attitude. But on Monday of the third week, it came to a head.

Felicia walked into the office with Declan after a long day of cutting, arranging, and delivering floral arrangements to a church, funeral home, and an anniversary party in Riverbend. Her temper was frayed. Especially since it had been twenty-one days, four hours, and twenty minutes since they'd kissed and twenty-one days, three hours, and ten minutes since he'd declared his firm position of remaining platonic. "Can I see the numbers for this month, please?" Felicia sat down at the oversize wooden desk that Declan had refurbished last week. The man never stopped working.

Lacey huffed. "Why? Don't you think I'm good at my job?"

"Enough." Felicia pinched the bridge of her nose, trying to release some of the tension from her poor, throbbing head. "I'm the owner of the company, and I asked to see the books."

Lacey shot up, opened a drawer and tossed papers onto the desk, but they blew all over the floor. "Here. I know Declan has you convinced I'm not good so he can replace me."

"Stop. I mean it. This ends now." Felicia had never heard herself speak in such a harsh tone, but it was time. Time to stop being generous and expect a little cooperation in return. This girl didn't seem to understand negotiations or working with others. This wasn't the girl she'd hired three years ago.

"Fine." Lacey shot from the room, knocking her shoulder into Declan, who didn't even budge.

Felicia dropped her head into her hands and stayed there for several minutes, willing the world to slow down and stop beating her against the proverbial walls of life. Declan didn't move, didn't retreat, but didn't advance either. He had been a human fly on the wall, watching everything and providing no opinion, for weeks.

After a few minutes, Felicia found the energy to get off the stool and gather the papers. He was quickly at her side, kneeling on the floor to help. It was the closest he'd been to her in forever in the spot where they'd kissed. "Maybe I should go after her."

"No," he said firmly but with no malice.

She sat back on her heels. "Why not?"

"Because you need to stop chasing and let her come around on her own. Besides, these aren't even related to the finances of your business. That's all on your computer."

Then he froze, like an ice statue in the middle of the Arctic, his expression turning even more thoughtful. "You can't change someone. They have to change themselves." His words sounded weighted, serious. "I'm working on something, Felicia." He wilted, as if left in the heat too long, but reached out, grazing her pinky with his own. "I'm working on something for you. To make me worthy. I tried to remain distant, but I can't deny how I feel about you, so my only option is to become the man you deserve."

EIGHTEEN

For another week, Declan applied for jobs every time he could find a minute to work in the office on Felicia's computer. He'd put together his resume and reached out to a few colleagues in New York, asking about any work in Tennessee. To his relief there was a message from his college roommate.

I believe you're innocent. No way you were stealing money. Let me make some calls. I'm glad you finally reached out to me for help. Sorry I never came to visit. I should have.

He didn't want to allow the man's words to give him hope or give him peace of mind that someone other than Felicia believed in his innocence. He'd fought so long to take the fall for his father. He'd never stopped fighting. He wanted to protect his mother and never let her know the truth, but they were all the two of them had left in the world. It was time to face her, even if she refused to see him. He needed to move forward and leave the past behind, but he couldn't do that without reconciling with family. No, it was more than that... He'd always wanted to introduce the woman he cared about to his mother. He couldn't do that, not now, not with his mother's hatred toward him.

For the first time since leaving prison, he thought about the future and believed in possibilities. A real life, not just survival. He loved working at the nursery, and it broke his heart to leave, but he couldn't be with a woman if he couldn't offer to be an equal partner. Once he'd worked on his relationship with his mother and found a job, he'd be better deserving of a girl like Felicia. He had to clean up his messes, if not for himself than for her.

He'd finished all the planting and work for the day, and Felicia was out with her friends, whisked away by Carissa an hour ago and not expected home until dinnertime, so today would be the day he'd take the first step forward. It would take a few hours, and it most likely would be a wasted trip since his mother would probably send him away, if she even remembered who he was, but he'd go anyway.

A message popped up on the screen for Lacey. She'd obviously forgotten to log out of an app.

Need more money for us to be together.

His fingers froze midstrike of a key. No. No. No. He didn't see that. It didn't mean anything. Yet, the hair on the back of his neck stood stiffer and taller than a redwood. He couldn't ignore the warning, so he clicked on the icon and up popped messages between her and who he assumed was Jason. The more he scrolled, the more his chest burned and his muscles tightened.

Jason: Sorry 4 hurting you, but U know I can't stand not making money 4 us.

Lacey: I don't care about money.

Jason: We need it for a place to live.

Lacey: You want to live with me?

Jason: It's all I want.

Lacey: How much do we need?

Jason: Only need a little for security deposit. I have most. Can you get...

Declan scrolled down, scanning the manipulative exchange

between Jason and Lacey. The man was beyond ruthless, toying with her emotions. He'd never wanted to punch a man out so badly in his life.

"What are you doing on the computer?" Lacey marched in and flipped the screen around before Declan could stop her.

"You had no right. This is personal." Lacey shoved into him, but his chair didn't budge, so she leaned across him to the keyboard and closed out the application.

Declan shook his head. "I know you don't like me, but please listen to me. That man is manipulating you. He's tugging on your emotions to get what he wants, and when you can't give it to him anymore, he'll be gone."

"That's you, not Jason. Jason loves me." Lacey's lip trembled, telling Declan she already suspected as much.

"I didn't mean to pry. The screen popped up while I was answering some emails. Listen, I know you want me gone, and I think that's partly because you think I'm bad for Felicia."

"You are." Lacey swiped two tears away that had pooled in the corner of her eyes. "You have nerve criticizing and accusing my boyfriend when you're an ex-con yourself with no future. Jason has plans. He's staring a company, and that's why he doesn't have money to get us a place. Now he does."

A sinking destroyer warning alarm went off in his head—loud, red, and frightening. He knew he shouldn't ask. He willed himself not to ask, but he had no choice. "Where did you get the money from, Lacey?"

Her shoulders straightened, her arms lengthened by her side, and she fisted her hands. With a gaze like a superhero firing lasers from her eyes, she crinkled her nose and said, "None of your business, and if you take this any further, I'll send you back to jail. I know I can. Jason told me you're a man with a noose around your neck, waiting to swing."

"Colorful boyfriend you have there." He tried to keep his

voice calm and low, but the threats she was making were dangerous. "You don't have to be concerned about me. I won't cause any trouble for you. I only wish you could see Jason for who he is and not let him hurt you anymore."

"Hurt me? He loves me," she said, despite the slight discoloration that still remained at the edge of her cheek from the bruises. "I told you he made a mistake and he's making it right."

He couldn't warn her any more, not when she hated him. She needed to hear the words from someone else. He'd tell Nana or Felicia about what was going on. "I'll be back in a few hours. If you see Felicia when she returns from her girls' outing, please let her know. I'll leave her a note, too."

With those words, he went inside the house to find Nana resting on the couch. "I'm leaving a note for Felicia on the kitchen table to let her know I'm borrowing the truck. I hate to leave like this, but I'd like to go visit someone. I'll be back by dinner."

"Okay, hon. Good luck and be safe."

He went to Nana's side, finding her a little pale. "When's the nurse getting here?"

"Oh, any minute. Don't worry about me. I'm just a little tired today, that's all." Nana waved him away, but he kissed her forehead.

"Get some rest."

After his shower, he dressed in the best clothes he owned, knowing his mother had always liked him clean cut and shaved. Clad in khaki pants and a button-up shirt, he drove through town and out the other side, feeling a sense of leaving home when he took the turn toward Riverbend. It would be a long day, but excitement stirred inside him. Excitement of possibilities that Felicia had made him believe in. The way she looked at him made him feel worthy. Worthy of everything he ever wanted. And he wanted a life with Felicia.

When he reached the memory care facility his mother had to live in after Zach had stolen all her money, he pulled into a space and longed to help her more. Perhaps if the job hunt turned out, he could pay for a better facility.

The minute he put the truck in Park, his nerves switched on injecting him with adrenaline. His heart raced and his breathing quickened. He'd faced fights over food, been shanked, threatened, beaten, but he'd never felt like this through any of that time.

He gripped the dashboard and hung his head, forcing his mind and body to slow. The idea of turning around and heading home without facing his mother drove him from the truck and into the front lobby.

"Can I help you, sir? Are you okay?" the young receptionist asked, as if he were a patient.

He cleared his throat and forced out the words. "I'm here to see Mary Mills. She's my mother." The sign on the desk said ID required, so he pulled his driver's license out and handed it to the woman.

The lady searched through a list on the table and then picked up the phone.

"I should tell you that my mother may refuse to see me. She's suffering from significant dementia, and I haven't tried to visit her for a while. Not since I caused her agitation last time I tried to see her."

The woman set the phone down and came around the corner, handing him back his ID, which he shoved into his front pocket. She slipped her hand into the crook of his arm. "Don't be so stressed. We deal with this often. Please don't take it personally if your mother yells or curses at you. She's not the person you once knew. It's not your fault. I'm sure deep down she'd love to see you. I'll take you to the nurses' station, and they can apprise you of her mood today. Sometimes residents have great days. You never know. She might remember you and welcome you with open arms."

He doubted that, but he kept his mouth closed, feeling like he'd just broken into Fort Knox without causing any commotion. The men and women dressed in scrubs behind a square counter in the center of a hallway looked up from their work with a welcoming smile.

"Hello! Who's going to have a special visitor today?"

Realizing the young man was speaking to him, Declan cleared his throat and said, "Mary Mills. That is, if she's up for a visit. I mean, I don't want to agitate her. I could even peek in on her and she doesn't have to know that I'm here." Coward. He was already backpedaling his way out the door.

"Don't be silly. Mary's having a pleasant time right now in our garden. She enjoys painting in the shade. Are you family?"

Declan nodded. "Her son."

"This is so good to hear. We were under the impression she had no family around here. She hasn't had a visitor since I started working here a few months ago."

"I've been away." It wasn't a lie. Felicia was right. He didn't have to tell everyone he'd served time as if he shouted his own version of a scarlet letter.

The man with a name tag stating Peter opened a door at the edge of the counter and came out. "Follow me."

The hallway smelled of sour milk and disinfectant, but there were no dirt smudges, cobwebs, or any other nightmarish things he'd imagined. Their soft steps echoed, as did a deep groan from one of the rooms.

"Don't mind Mr. Shelton. He's a little dramatic. He taught theater at the university for years." Peter used his badge to open the door at the end of the corridor that exited into a sunny, vibrant garden that Felicia would approve of if she were here.

Declan caught sight of his mother sitting in a chair painting.

His pulse pumped hot blood through his body, as if preparing for a riot in the prison yard. The memory of her harsh words and yelling in front of the neighbors and friends froze him at the threshold to the garden.

When Peter reached his mother's side and whispered something to her, he turned and waved him over, but Declan couldn't move.

Fear locked him in place, keeping him safe from the one thing that broke his heart more than anything had to date in his life—his own mother hating him. He didn't blame her. It wasn't her fault. She didn't know the truth, and she was ill. They'd once been so close, though.

Peter joined him again. "It's okay. She's having a good day, and the medication the doctors have her on has been keeping her lucid and calm. I'm guessing, like many of our incoming patients, she was combative prior to her arrival. I assure you, she will not be that way today."

His words promised the possibility not of reconciliation but of a chance at a conversation. A chance for him to tell the truth. Or should he keep the secret to protect his father's memory and try to rebuild what he could with his mother? He forced himself into action and joined his mother, sitting at her side.

When he looked up, he noticed Peter had gone. Only one staff member sitting almost concealed by a fern in the corner remained as witness if his mother attacked him with her fists again. He forced a breath in and said, "Hello, Mother. It's me, your son, Declan."

She calmly placed her paintbrush on the easel. "Well, it's about time you came to visit me. I thought I'd done a better job of raising you than that."

Declan blinked. What kind of medicine had they prescribed, or had her dementia taken hold and kept the memories she didn't want from her mind?

"I can't blame you. After..." Her voice cracked, but she cleared her throat and looked at him with the same cloudy eyes he remembered. "After I sent you away. You must realize I was confused."

"No, Mama. You had a right to be angry at me. I'm so sorry that I wasn't there to protect you from Zach. You wouldn't be here if I—"

"Hadn't gone to jail to save your father's life?" She smiled, and the perpendicular lines around her lips deepened. "For a time, anyway."

His mouth fell open, but he had no words to say. A bird swooped and landed in a nearby tree, insects chirped, the smell of paint infiltrated his senses, but he couldn't process anything else.

Mama's hand settled on his. "Listen, your father confessed on his deathbed that he was the one who'd embezzled the money. He was in over his head in gambling debts, and when they came to collect, they threatened you and me." She sighed. "I'm afraid I didn't see the truth in time. Then after his death and your incarceration, I was weak. I slipped into a dark place, and that's when Zach Frayser entered my life, dragging me from my depression. He claimed to be an attorney and wanted to help get you out of jail." She scooted closer and gripped his fingers. "I thought Zach was helping me. That's how he stole all my money. I was paying him to get you out of jail. I blamed your father for being weak and dumb, but I was the dumb one."

"No, don't say that." Declan kissed his mother's hand. "He was highly manipulative. That's why I finally got you into this place. I'm sorry it isn't better. I didn't have any money or a job."

"Are you kidding? I love this place." She lit up like a lightning bug on a dark night illuminating the world.

Declan held tight to his mother, wishing they had more time together. "I'm going to make everything better for you, for Felicia, for myself. It's time for me to get my life back, Mom. It's time to let go of the past."

"Felicia?"

A swell of happiness made him feel as if he'd burst. "Yes, she's a woman you would adore. I can't wait to bring her here to meet you."

"No." She slipped her hands away and sat back.

He watched her turn from welcoming and loving to rigid and distant. "I don't understand."

"No, you don't." She picked up her paintbrush and dipped it into daffodil yellow. "I've seen you, and we've made our peace. Now, it's time for you to go."

"But I just got here."

"You need to leave. And you won't bring Felicia back for a visit. I wish you all the best, but this is it. Now, go and never visit me again. I've done enough to you. It's your turn to have a life."

NINETEEN

The sun was already resting along the tree line, ready to say good night, when Carissa pulled into Felicia's driveway. Although Felicia had enjoyed the afternoon with the girls, she was eager to return home.

"So are you glad now that we kidnapped you for a few hours?" Carissa drove to the front of the house and took the spot where Felicia's truck normally sat. Great. She hoped Lacey hadn't snuck off to see Jason.

"Yes, it was nice."

"Nice?" Carissa put the car into park and sighed. "Listen, I know Jackie gave you the third degree, but in the end, she came around about Declan."

"Did she?" Felicia tilted her head down and looked up with her best you're-joking expression.

"Okay, well, she took a step in the right direction."

"Was that before or after she summoned Davey inside Maple Grounds and told him to get the tar ready?"

Carissa smirked. "But then when he went to get the Elders together to run Declan out of town, Jackie calmed him down.

She likes to make sure everyone believes she's in control, that's all."

"I get it. I do."

"Only you, Felicia." Carissa chuckled. "You're a saint. I would've been stomping off or avoiding her. Not you. Always the diplomat."

"I know she acts this way because she cares about me. It's just that I want all of you to like Declan. Could you convince them to come here for dinner one evening? I know he'll win them over if they spend some time with him."

Carissa nodded. "Sure. I can do that. Are you ready for Jackie to be near Declan, though?"

"I'll prep him. Don't worry. Have you seen the guy? I think his great-grandfather was a giant."

"A giant underwear model with muscles, amazing hair, and broad chest. There's no doubt to any of us about his physical appeal." Carissa waggled her brows.

"I saw him in boxers once. Will I ever live that down? He's more than just attractive in a carnal sense. He's deep, thoughtful, attentive, and puts me before himself. That's what this is all about. I know it is. He's protecting me from people's prejudice. He doesn't seem to understand I've dealt with that my entire life."

"I know. But that's what's made you so strong and diplomatic." Carissa traced the stitching in the steering wheel. "How are things between you? Is he still being cold and distant?"

"He says he's working on something so we can be together, but each time we're near each other he's like an iceberg on Mars."

"Ouch." Carissa continued her study along the leather until she dropped her hands to her sides. "You sure he's going to come around? I mean, I don't want you pining for someone who will never be available. You're too good for that."

"Now you sound like Jackie."

"She has a point."

Felicia threw her hands up. "Great, the world is coming to an end. You just sided with Judas Jackie."

"That's all behind us now."

"Really? So if you saw her talking to Drew alone in a dark alley, you wouldn't plot her demise?"

Carissa gripped the steering wheel again, this time as if she were going to bolt across town and run Jackie down. "I might order some tar myself." She took a long breath. "But she wouldn't do that. Her fiancé-stealing days were a youthful indiscretion that she won't repeat. She'd never even flirt with Drew."

"That sounded like a quote straight from Ms. Horton." Felicia opened her door, eager to find Declan and tell him it was time to let go of his fears and give them a chance. He was ready to hear it now—or at least she was ready to make him hear it.

"Wait." Carissa touched her arm to stay her movements. "You know I'm on your side, right? I'll bring the girls over for dinner whenever you want."

"I know. Thanks." Felicia slid out of the car and shut the door, offered a friendly wave bye, and then darted to the house to face Declan. After a moment to collect her courage, she opened the door and found the room dark. No sign of him or anyone. No delicious aroma, no sizzling meat, no smiles. "Declan? Nana? Lacey?"

No one answered. She made her way into the living room and shut the door. "Hello?"

Lacey stepped out of her room into the hall. Felicia was relieved to see her. Maybe she really had given up on Jason.

"Where is everyone?"

The light flooded out of Lacey's room, showing her eyeing the floor. "Nana's asleep, has been since I came in from work."

"And Declan?"

Lacey slid her toes back and forth on the carpet. "I don't want to say."

Felicia stiffened at Lacey's serious tone. "Just tell the truth. That's all that matters."

"The truth is, I don't know. One minute he was on your computer. I think he was digging into the finance stuff like I'm sure you asked him to, but I'm not positive. When I walked in, he shut the computer off fast and then took off in the truck without a word." Lacey inched closer. "I'm sure he'll be back any minute. He's been gone for hours."

"Hours?"

"Yes."

Felicia eyed the door. "Okay, well, thanks for letting me know."

"I'm sure he has a good reason. I mean, he'll tell you when he returns. Just make sure you listen between his words and watch his expression. It's something I learned from your grand-mother. When a man is lying or keeping things from you or he doesn't want to tell you too much. I'm sure Declan will explain, though. You trust him, right?"

"Yes, of course I do." Felicia didn't like where this was going, probably based on some jealousy on her part, and she'd punished Lacey enough. "Listen, tomorrow I'll need you all day. If you could run out and purchase some things for me, I'll leave the list on the desk along with the company card."

Lacey bolted forward. "Thank you. I really appreciate this. I'm so glad we're friends again. It means everything to me." She bit her bottom lip then looked up at Felicia with the most honest expression she'd ever seen in her cousin. "I miss you. I miss the way things were between us."

"Me, too."

Lacey launched into a hug and clung to Felicia. They stood there for a minute or two as if her hug meant the end to all the drama and a hope for a better relationship between them. It felt right, like the way it used to be between them.

Lights flashed through the house from the end of the driveway, drawing Felicia to the window. Her truck bounced along the gravel and stopped in her spot. She swallowed the feeling of suspicion. "I'm sure you've worked hard. Why don't you go get cleaned up while I get dinner ready."

Lacey eyed the window. "Right. Sure. I'll give you two some privacy." She darted to her room and shut the door. It was nice to have the old, sweet, caring Lacey back. Felicia had always known separating her from Jason would make all the difference in her attitude.

Felicia couldn't stand still, so she went to the refrigerator and pulled out some hotdogs and tossed them in a frying pan. The front door opened, and before he even said a word, she could smell the aroma of men's cologne. A scent he hadn't worn around her before. It was cedar with an undertone of allure.

"I'm sorry I'm late. It took longer than I thought. You don't have to cook. I've got it. I'll whip something up quick."

She grabbed a fork out of the drawer and flipped the hot dogs. "No need. I just arrived home and found my truck gone and didn't know where you went or when you'd be home, so I figured I better get some dinner ready."

"You didn't get my note?" Declan eyed the kitchen table. "I left it here."

"There wasn't any message that I found." Felicia heard the air of agitation in her voice, but she couldn't help it.

He searched the table and then the counter. Brushing past her, he ignited the hair on her arms to full attention. "Here it is. Weird. It's behind the bills on the stand. Who would put it there?"

"What did it say?" she asked. A hint of comfort that he'd cared enough to leave her a message helped ease her nerves.

"It said that I was going out and borrowing the truck. I hoped that was okay and that I'd be back by dinner." Declan moved behind her, close, so close, his hands on her shoulders. "I'm so sorry if I worried you. Didn't Nana tell you I'd left?"

"No, she's asleep." Felicia knew she had no reason to be mad at him. He'd left a message and told her grandmother. "Where did you go?"

Silence.

Felicia moved the pan away from the flame and turned off the burner. "I think I have a right to know where you took my truck. I'd thought Lacey had stolen it to go visit Jason."

"No. I borrowed it." He rested his chin on the top of her head. "What's wrong? You sound different."

"Nothing's wrong. I'm fine. I just wanted to know where you went, but if you're going to keep it from me..."

"I'm not. I mean, I am for a few days." He turned her into his arms, his eyes longing and searching. "I told you that I couldn't be with you because I can't be the man you deserve, but something's changed. No, you changed me. I'm working on something, and I want to tell you when I have it all worked out. As for today..." He blinked and looked away. "I went to River-bend. I needed to see someone." He released her and retrieved the plates from the cabinet.

"Who?" Perhaps it was her frustration about how far he'd been from her for weeks, or maybe it was Lacey's words haunting her about spotting signs when a man was doing wrong. Either way, she wanted answers.

He set the plates onto the table and leaned over with his palms pressed to the wood top. "I...I went to see my mother."

"Your mother? I thought you two weren't on speaking terms." She flinched at how insensitive her words were.

"We're not. I mean, we weren't, but we spoke, and now we're not speaking again." Declan pushed from the table and set a plate at each seat. "Can we not talk about that right now?" He sounded wounded, lost, and it tugged at her heart. She wanted to race over and hug him, but something still stood in the way.

"I just need a few days to work some things out, and then if everything does, I want to ask you out on a real date."

The way he said he wanted to ask her on a date sounded distant, hollow. "I'm not forcing you to ask me out. Don't do me any favors."

"You know I want to be with you, Felicia," he said in a deep, wanting tone.

"How would I know that?" Her patience snapped, and she had no diplomacy left. "I feel like a rubber band being stretched between two realities. One, you want me and one you don't. First you say you can't be with me, then you act like you do, then you don't, and now you do. It's been weeks of tiptoeing around with desire floating in the air between us. A brush of your arm against my skin, a breath over my cheek, a longing glance, but not one kiss not since the one you planted on me that spun me around and had me believing you were opening up to me. Now you're closed off more than ever."

"I do want you. More than anything." He grabbed hold of her and held her tight against his chest, looking down at her with fire in his eyes. "I know I haven't been fair to you. It's been complicated, but I wanted to wait until I had everything worked out before I told you how I really felt." He took in a deep, stuttered breath and slid his fingers into her hair, clutching the back of her neck. "That I am falling for you. That you're the most beautiful, accomplished, talented, giving, lovable human being I've ever met. And there is nothing more in life that I want to do than kiss you."

TWENTY

A week was too long to wait for the job interview and to keep the secret from Felicia, but he worried that he'd get her hopes up and then let her down. He'd come close to giving in, succumbing to his passion. He closed his eyes and savored the memory of the way she'd looked at him, the way she'd clung to him, the way she crumbled when he released her without committing. It gutted him, tore him up with need and want and desire and he'd dreamed about their almost kiss every night since. There were many things in the world he could face, but seeing Felicia disappointed wasn't one of them. When he kissed her again, he wanted it to be a kiss sealing their future, not their end.

He stood at the window waiting for Stella to pick Felicia up for all-day wedding planning, filming segment, and other distractions for Operation Secret Job Interview. The girls had been more than kind and supported him on his wishes and even encouraged him to get his life together before pursuing Felicia. If they still had an issue with him having romantic intentions for her, they didn't share it with him. Except for Stella. She always had a sassy remark to make when they were on the phone, but he started to realize that was only a form of communication for her.

Stella's old 1957 Chevy pulled in with a new paint job. The girl had refurbished the car to look brand-new yet classic, with the turquoise paint and white-walled tires. He held his breath and watched Felicia get into the car and ride away from the house. Hopefully, when she returned, he could tell her about the job and they could move forward. If not, he'd get another interview. He wouldn't give up, not until he could earn the right to date Felicia and get the town's approval. He looked forward to stopping by the center to see his mother on his way to his interview. She'd been so determined to drive him out of her life. Did she still hate him, despite saying she believed that he'd protected them by going to jail instead of his father? If not, why had she called for the staff member to escort him away so quickly?

With mutant, four winged butterflies in his chest, he stepped out of the camper and headed to the office to get the keys to the truck and to call the center to see if he could visit. When he rounded the corner of the house, he heard voices—Lacey and a man he'd never heard before.

"We have to do something," the deep voice said with an air of agitation.

"What?" Lacey sounded winded, scared.

Declan bolted into the office and found who he guessed to be Jason gripping Lacey by the arms. "Take your hands off her."

The young man jumped back but then recovered. He flipped his long hair out of his eyes and squared his shoulders, but his hands shook. "This is none of your business."

"It's my business if you put your hands on Lacey," Declan said in his deep, intimidating tone, fisting his hands at his sides.

Lacey leapt between them. "Nothing's going on. Jason came by to see me, that's all. I'll walk him out."

"There's no car here," Declan pointed out, knowing Jason probably left his car hidden. Couldn't Lacey see him for the coward he was?

"I told him to park out of sight. I knew you'd act all crazy." Lacey tugged Jason to the door. "Stay out of my business. You're not my father."

Declan turned to face them when they moved around him. "No—if I was, I'd call the police and have Jason removed from my property."

Lacey huffed. "Not your property, and you're no friend to the police."

She had a point, and he had no right to interfere, but he'd share this with Felicia the minute he saw her again. For now, he needed to get to his appointment, so he snagged the keys and raced to the truck. He only had a few hours to make it to River-bend, do the interview, see his mother, and get to the house before Felicia returned. Luckily, Stella, Carissa, and Nana all knew of his plans. He'd enjoyed getting closer to all of them, knowing how important they were to Felicia.

Luckily, the traffic was light, and he made it to Riverbend in record time. The clock tower in the center of campus struck ten, so he had thirty minutes to get to the interview. He wished he had a coat and tie, but he'd have to make do with his khakis and button-up shirt for now.

His pulse matched his quick steps down the main street to the four-story, brick-front building. It was only the human resources building, since most of the people worked remotely, which made the job all the more appealing to Declan. Talk about the best of both worlds, remaining at the nursery to help out in the mornings and evenings around his day job.

The two front glass doors opened into a small lobby with an exposed brick wall behind a receptionist desk, where a woman waited with a warm smile. "Mr. Mills?"

"Yes, ma'am." He stood tall and matched her smile.

"Great. Follow me, please." Her heels clicked around the desk and down the hallway to a conference room, where she directed him to sit at a long table. "They'll be in to see you shortly."

"Thank you." He paced around the table, then sat, then stood, then looked out the window, and then sat again. All the time, his heart beat against his chest and his mouth turned drier than dirt during a ten-year drought.

Twenty-two minutes later, two suits walked in, and he couldn't help but flash back to his pre-prison days, when he wore the same coat-and-tie uniform to work each day. At that moment, he realized he didn't miss it. He enjoyed getting his hands dirty and working outside.

The front man set a laptop on the table and held his hand out. Declan shook it and then the other when the second man held it out.

"Sit, please." The front man with the red tie pointed to a chair, so Declan settled into it. He opened the laptop, scrolled through something, and then closed it and folded his hands. "We're impressed with your resume, and we value Mr. Hutchins, who spoke on your behalf," he said in a condescending, this-is-just-a-formality kind of tone.

"But..." Declan offered, knowing this wasn't going to be all he'd hoped.

"Can we be honest?" The second man sat forward, clasping his hands like the other.

"You can't hire an ex-con," Declan blurted.

Both men shifted, as if the term made them so uncomfortable they didn't want to hear it aloud. "The thing is that we're a small company that allows our employees a certain amount of... freedom. That means we don't have the resources to monitor any single employee, especially one who is working as a senior accountant."

Declan felt his dreams of a better life slipping away. Felicia slipping away. "I would be fine with a junior level spot, in more of a supportive role."

"As we said, we're a small company."

The firm tone brooked no more argument. Declan wouldn't bother protesting his innocence. Their you're-not-worth-our-time-or-effort expressions spoke volumes. "I see. Thank you for taking the meeting," he said, but what he wanted to say was thanks for wasting his time.

After a quick good-bye, Declan hotfooted it across town, anger bubbling to the surface with the realization that he'd gotten ahead of himself. The life he wanted wouldn't be so easy to achieve.

Disappointment rained on his day, but he refused to let it win, so he headed to visit his mother. But when he entered, the receptionist stood with a hesitant, pouty-lip expression. She didn't have to tell him. He knew. His mother refused to see him.

Dejected, frustrated, and upset, he marched to the truck, and found an officer standing beside it. He forced a calming breath, concentrating on the fact that not every law enforcement officer was out to put him back in jail. "I apologize, Officer. I thought I was allowed to park here. I'll move now."

"I need to see your license and registration, please," the policeman ordered.

"I'm sorry?"

The officer moved his hand to his gun. "Is this your vehicle, sir?"

"No, I borrowed it."

Another officer came up behind him with his hand on his weapon. "You sure you borrowed it?"

"Yes, why?"

"Because this vehicle was reported stolen."

TWENTY-ONE

A friendship circle surrounded Felicia in the heart of Maple Grounds. She held her phone tight in her hands. "I don't understand."

Jackie uncharacteristically patted her leg. "Maybe it's for the best."

"No. It doesn't make sense. Why was he arrested? Why in Riverbend, and why do they want me to report to the precinct?"

Stella looked to Carissa with an I-know-something look.

"What?" Felicia shot forward. "You're keeping something from me."

Mary-Beth cleared her throat. "We were helping Declan make a better life. He wanted to surprise you."

"You were in on this, too?" Felicia shot Mary-Beth a sideways glance.

"I wasn't." Jackie glowered at them all. "What's going on? Spill it now."

Stella cracked her knuckles. "We were trying to help the man you claim to care about so that you'd have a better life with him. He was in Riverbend for a job interview. An old college roommate made a call, and he wanted to keep it a secret until he knew it would work out. He didn't want to get your hopes up because he knew you were frustrated with the back and forth of everything."

"Not of his circumstances. Of his lack of trust in me. The fact that he wouldn't share things with me, that he kept pulling away."

"We're sorry. We thought we were helping." Carissa studied her hands. "We should never keep secrets from each other."

"You're right, you shouldn't." Jackie sat up superiorly tall.

"It's okay. I understand that you were trying to help." Felicia sighed.

"That's your problem. That's how you end up with all these strays. You're too nice and too giving. This man isn't right for you. For goodness' sakes, he's in jail." Jackie shot up from her chair. "I, for one, am not going to support this another minute. You should leave him in jail and return home to your life." Jackie gathered her purse and marched out the door.

"I need a ride, please." Felicia looked to Stella.

"On it." Before anyone could say another word, Stella was out front with the car started.

Mary-Beth wrapped her arms around Felicia. "We're here to support you. We trust you, so ignore Jackie. Go figure out what's going on before you make any decisions."

Felicia slipped from her arms and joined Stella with Carissa by her side. "You don't have to go."

"I'm part of this. I'm going." Carissa hopped into the back seat, and they took off for Riverbend. To Felicia's relief, they rode in silence all the way, allowing her to think through everything. How could she continue caring about a man who didn't confide in her? Jackie was right that she needed to stick up for herself and stop allowing strays to take advantage of her. She didn't want to live a life with secrets and deception. He had to trust her, or he had to go. It would kill her, but enough was enough.

They pulled up to the precinct, and Felicia marched inside, determined to give Declan a piece of her mind and then some. She signed in and paced the lobby, Stella and Carissa sitting nearby, still quiet.

The wait felt like a week until the door opened and a man in uniform waved her back into the heart of the building. Stella and Carissa were at her heels, protecting her the way they'd protected each other ever since they were young. They all settled into a small office with an oversized wooden desk.

"Ms. Hughes, we apologize for the inconvenience, but when you reported your truck stolen, we thought it best to have you come to the station, since the man in question stated you'd allowed him to borrow the vehicle. If you could just give us your official statement, show us your driver's license and registration, we can give you the keys and you can be on your way."

"I didn't report the truck stolen," she blurted, stunned by the man's words.

The officer lifted the edge of a paper and studied the next page. "He stated that he borrowed the truck."

"No," she mumbled. "I mean, yes."

"Which is it?" The officer had an air of irritation in his voice.

Carissa raised her hand, as if in class. "He's an employee and he has free access to the truck at any time."

"Is that the case, Ms. Hughes?" the officer asked.

"Yes." Felicia sucked in a quick breath and looked the man in the eyes. "Yes, that's true. I'm not sure who made this report, and I apologize for any inconvenience. But I assure you, it wasn't me."

"I see." The officer slid the piece of paper back.

"So, can I see Declan now?" Felicia asked, eager to tell him she hadn't reported him for stealing anything and to reprimand him for keeping secrets.

"He's in violation of his parole."

"But he didn't steal the truck," Felicia reminded him.

The officer tapped a pen against the desk. "Are you family?"

"No, he, um...works for me. Like we told you." Felicia knotted her purse strap in her lap.

"If I can give you a piece of advice, ma'am... Mr. Mills may not be the best person to work for you. He has a history with the law."

"Yes, I'm well aware of his history," Felicia said, feeling anger simmer at yet another person judging Declan without knowing him.

The officer frowned and cleared his throat. "If you don't want to press charges or file a report on him, then my hands are tied. Give me a minute to take care of some paperwork, and he'll be released. He'll need to call his probation officer to follow up since we notified him of the arrest."

Felicia's stomach twisted. "I'll make sure to tell him that Declan did nothing wrong."

The officer strutted out the door. "If you say so."

Stella stood with arms crossed in the corner. "Who would report your truck stolen?"

"I don't know. I hope Declan doesn't think that it was me."

Carissa scooted her chair closer. "He wouldn't. But I have to ask you, Felicia. Are you sure this is the man you want in your life? A man who will always be someone everyone sees as a felon? Can you handle that kind of prejudice?"

Felicia rolled her head to the side and gave her an are-you-serious look. "In first grade, I was called confused colored. In third, Milky Milano. By junior high school, they became more creative with Oreo, zebra, dalmatian, checkerboard, penguin, and swirl girl. Oh, and my personal favorite, which only took nine years for kids to come up with, was Panda Princess. Do you honestly think I can't handle a little prejudice in my life?"

"You should've let me punch them on the playground like I wanted," Stella said with full-blown sass.

Felicia shook her head. "That wouldn't have solved anything, and you would've been in more trouble. Violence was never the answer." She thought of all the taunting for a moment and realized how Stella always had her back. "But I appreciated knowing you were willing to get in trouble to save my honor. You four have been everything to me."

"And you've been that for us. That's the only reason we worry. Because we care." Carissa threw her arms around Felicia.

They huddled for a second with Stella managing to put a hand on their backs for her awkward but loving comfort. "Who do you think called the cops, anyway?"

Stella's question hung in the air for a moment. "Did Nana know about today? Maybe she thought it had been stolen. Although, I doubt it. Declan and Nana have gotten close. He would've told her that he was taking it."

"Then who else could it be?" Carissa asked.

"Lacey and Jason." Declan's voice drew their attention to the doorway. "Although, I will confess that for a moment, I thought perhaps your friends had set me up."

Carissa shot up from the chair. "We wouldn't do that."

Stella put a hand in front of her. "Down girl. I'm the fighter here." She walked up to Declan in true Stella style. "I would've thought the same, but for future reference, Carissa's right." She smacked him on the shoulder and strutted past him. "Come on, Carissa. We should wait in the lobby. Let's give these two a chance to chat." She paused. "But after that, I want to know more about this Lacey-Jason situation."

Declan nodded, and Carissa hurried out the door behind Stella, leaving Felicia to face him.

"This all could've been avoided if you had told me what you were doing." She started to close her mouth, but once she started talking, it was as if she couldn't stop. Diplomacy had been left in Sugar Maple. "You say you trust me, but you don't. I don't even know why you need another job. You have one. I thought you were happy there. Why do you have to go get one this far away? Is it me? Do you want to put some distance between us because you realized you don't really want to move things between us forward?"

Tears pricked in the corner of her eyes and her body shook, upset about the truck, his arrest, the secrets, Lacey, and everything else that was going on.

Declan grabbed the doorframe, as if holding himself up. His tone of voice was incredulous when he asked, "Do I want to leave? Do I not want to be with you?"

She nodded, unable to speak anymore.

"Felicia Hughes... This is how much I want to be with you." He closed the two steps between them, lifted her up into his arms with her toes off the floor, and kissed her. Madly, deeply, wildly, lovingly.

TWENTY-TWO

For three days, Declan enjoyed time alone with Felicia. He knew that tomorrow would bring a film crew to the nursery to finish the segment for the Knox Brevard show and, with it, everyone she cared about from town. He only hoped he could show them how much he tried to make Felicia happy. If only he had a job to support her like he was raised to do. After finishing repairs on the outer fence, he showered and then raced to the house. He found Nana asleep on the couch, so he tucked her in for her afternoon nap, packed a picnic, and took it out to the heart of the property in back at a small hill, under a beautiful dogwood tree that was in full bloom.

"Whatcha got there?" Felicia tilted her sun hat up to her hairline, allowing him to see her vibrant eyes.

"Our lunch. I thought it might be nice to sit out here. Summer is heating up, and we won't have many more afternoons like this in our future." Declan hoped he hadn't overstepped. "I know it's not a real date, but I'm hoping to follow up on a lead next week in Creekside."

"A crowded restaurant in the heart of a big city isn't my idea of a date. This is perfect." She settled on the blanket he'd spread out, kneeling and then lowering to her hip. The woman was graceful even in galoshes and a wide-brimmed hat, which she removed and set by her side. "And I admit, your cooking is much better than any restaurant I've ever been to."

His face flushed. "Thanks. I hope you don't mind. I've planted some fresh vegetables behind the field in the back corner. If you need that land for anything, I'd be happy to rip it out."

"No, that's fine." She opened the basket and took a long sniff. "Wow, you spoil me."

"I try."

"Tell me something." Felicia removed her galoshes and then straightened her legs. "Why do you want to return to working as some corporate person? You seem so happy here in the fresh air."

He shrugged. "It's what I'm good at, and it pays the bills."

"Do you enjoy working in an office?" Felicia asked.

He thought about it for a moment and decided happiness would be a strong word. "It's as good as any job."

"But you smile, hum, and are happy here. Why do you have to find a job somewhere else?"

"Because I can't live off you, Felicia." He leaned in and caressed her soft cheek, willing her to understand. "I need to be a man. Perhaps it's old-fashioned, but I need a job, a way to make my own way in this world, or I'll never feel right about being anything more than your friend."

The way she stiffened at his words tortured him, but he couldn't lie. Not to her. Not ever. "Please, be patient. I'll figure things out. Don't give up on me, not yet."

"I won't. I believe in you, Declan." She closed her eyes and leaned into his hand. "But you still keep your distance from me. It's as if you keep all your passion inside until it explodes, and then you consume me with one kiss. It's amazing, and confusing, and I want more. I deserve more."

"You do," he whispered, as if the words were too painful to say loud enough for the world to hear.

Felicia leaned away from him and studied his expression, unnerving him a little. "I don't mean that I deserve *more* than you. I mean I deserve *all* of you."

"I know what you meant." He opened the picnic basket in an attempt to change the subject. "I was thinking about utilizing the vegetables to cook, and if they turn out well, perhaps I could sell them. I know it's your land, and of course the money's yours, but it couldn't hurt to expand the nursery, could it?"

"If the idea's yours and you do the work, I'll rent you the property. I've done it before."

"You have?"

"Yeah, there used to be a woman who thought all produce was poisoned by the government, so she rented an acre from us and planted her own food. Unfortunately, she died of cancer from smoking for fifty years."

"I'm sorry to hear that." His memories floated back to his cooking at the prison and how he longed for fresh produce for their meals. "Does Sugar Maple have a farm-to-table restaurant or market?"

"No." Felicia took a chicken salad sandwich from him—made with the tarragon he grew that she enjoyed—on a fresh brioche bun. "That sounds like an amazing idea."

"I've heard of them before. When I go to the grocery store, the organic section is so small. It would be nice to have that option for cooking. That's why I thought you should start your own little garden."

"It's your idea, your garden. You can have that back acre for whatever you want."

"I won't have time to keep up with it once I'm working a

new job, but maybe I can start it until then. Get it up and running, and then you can take it over."

"Okay, but you keep all the profits," she said flatly.

He couldn't—wouldn't—have that. "Nope, it's your land."

"As I said, you can rent it. I think one dollar a month should cover it." She smiled, so sweetly it almost soothed the knowledge that she was giving him a handout.

"What did you charge the woman who used to rent property from you before?"

"I charged her $30 a month," Felicia said with hesitation in her voice.

"That's awfully low," Declan accused. "I'll do $50 a month, starting."

She shot out her hand. "Deal."

He took it, kissed her knuckles and nuzzled her ear, pulling her close to him under the dogwood in the shade of summer. They playfully rolled about and teased one another like children, enjoyed their meal, and he never wanted lunch to end.

Each second he spent with Felicia was a gift straight from heaven. Hopefully, in a week or so, he could officially date her with the knowledge he could afford to take her out and treat her the way she deserved. The only problem besides getting the job was that his heart ached each time he thought about leaving her to go to work. Especially in Creekside. He'd have to move his camper between the two cities if he'd make it to work each day and only see Felicia on weekends, but it was a sacrifice he had no choice but to make.

After all, how many opportunities were out there for a man convicted of stealing money from his own father's company?

TWENTY-THREE

Dark clouds tumbled over the mountains, unloading torrential rain. Felicia pressed her nose to the window. "It hasn't rained like this in ten years. I hope the front field doesn't flood. That's the lowest part of the grounds."

Declan rubbed her shoulders, relieving tension near her neck. "Don't worry. It'll be fine. If it continues, I'll dig a trench and funnel the water to the ditch out to the road."

Nana yawned. "All this rain's making me tired. I'm headed to bed."

Felicia looked at her watch. "It's ten in the morning."

"I know, but can't an old lady nap when she wants?" She hobbled to her room and shut the door.

Declan abandoned her too, attempting to fix his tie again.

"I thought you were a big corporate guy. Didn't you wear a tie?"

"It's been years, and I want to look perfect. Apparently they're in desperate need of someone to help at a veterans center in Creekside. I'm supposed to meet with a James Benjamin. According to my friend, he's an amazing man, and he already knows my history. He doesn't care, as long as I'm able-bodied and willing to do more to help out than just work in finance. It's kind of an eclectic job, where I'll also do transportation, paperwork, intakes, billing, and acquisitions."

"Will this make you happy?" Felicia asked, not sure any of those jobs would get him to smile the way he did when he was working in his garden or with herbs.

"If I have money to support myself and perhaps help you someday, then I'll be happy."

She knew there was no changing his mind, so she adjusted his tie. He was set on the traditional male role in a relationship, and it was one of the things she loved about him, even if it frustrated her. Of course, she didn't want a man to mooch off her, but Declan would never do that. He worked harder than any man she'd ever known. The workload at the nursery had become bearable, and she hadn't been worried about Nana near as much. Selfish. That's what she was being. The man needed a job, and she wanted him to stay for her own selfish reasons. "You look handsome, professional, and capable. Good luck." She stood on her toes and kissed his cheek. "I have a good feeling about this for you."

He beamed with enthusiasm, and that warmed her heart. "I'll be gone until after dinner, so please don't let anyone report the truck missing." He winked, but his words tickled that niggling feeling about that scenario. "I had hoped to surprise you when I had a job, but I have to admit I like you in my corner better."

"Please be careful. The rain hasn't stopped, and the roads could be flooded. If you can't make it back today, don't try. I don't need the truck for a couple of days."

"Don't worry so much. Is this what it's going to be like when I go to work every day?" Declan teased, poking her in her ticklish spot.

"Yes, so get used to it."

"I can get used to anything with you." He kissed her, only a peck and nothing like before. Oh, how she longed for one of *those* kisses.

Declan left her with nothing but her thoughts, the rain pelting against the window and her grandmother sleeping. She'd never felt so alone. In all the time before Declan, she'd never needed anyone around. She was strong, independent, and liked her alone time. But if there was one thing that afternoon taught her, it was that her life had changed the minute Declan Mills drove into it. Now, she only hoped he'd stay. Job or no job, she wanted that man in her life.

In the late afternoon, Nana woke and they played cards, but Felicia couldn't focus. By dinnertime, she was checking her watch, waiting for him to return. As she cleared the dishes and helped Nana back to her room, there was a knock. She abandoned the cleaning and raced for the door, struggling between hope that Declan had landed the job and fear he'd done so.

But when she opened the door, it wasn't Declan but Lacey standing in the rain. Felicia thought about slamming the door in her face, but she couldn't. She could never turn her back on anyone who meant something to her. Everyone deserved some sort of grace. "Did he hurt you again?"

"No. Can I come inside?" Lacey held a folder to her chest and snugged the hood of her raincoat over her forehead.

"I guess, but I don't think you could convince me to give you your old job back. Not when you disappeared for so long."

"I'm not here about a job." Lacey removed her hood and sheepishly handed Felicia the folder she'd been clinging to. "I didn't know what to do. It's been tearing me up inside. You know I love you like a sister. That's why I left. I knew I couldn't stay and allow this to continue, but I didn't know how to tell you since I knew it would break your heart."

"What are you talking about?" Felicia opened the folder and

pulled out spreadsheets, documents, purchase orders, and credit card statements. "What's all this?"

"Proof," Lacey stated, as if that was supposed to mean something.

"Of what?" Felicia studied the documents, shoving plates out of the way and spreading the sheets of paper over the table.

"Of Declan stealing from you," Lacey said, tears in her eyes.

A lump of terror lodged in Felicia's suddenly dry throat, constricting her breathing. She pushed the purchase order out of the way and then pulled out the credit card statement. "You're mistaken. You have to be."

"I'm not. I printed these off as proof the day he ran off. I busted him digging through the computer in your office, and that's when I saw what he was doing. When I confronted him, I told him what he was doing was not only illegal but wrong to you. That I was going to tell. That's when he took off in your truck."

"You're the one who reported it stolen." Felicia wanted to yell and tell Lacey to leave her home and never return, but she couldn't. She needed to know more. To prove she was wrong, that Declan would never do such a thing.

"That's why I left. I knew you'd believe him over me, but not before I printed these off and had time to really study them. I even took them to a forensic accountant my mother knows. He confirmed what I suspected. Declan's been taking money from the nursery."

Lacey's words swept Felicia's knees out from under her, and she fell into the chair. There was no way any of this was real. It couldn't be. The mere idea of it was torture. "No. It's not true."

Lacey dug through the papers and withdrew a letter. "I knew you wouldn't believe me. You never believe me," she blubbered and tossed the paper at Felicia. "That's why I had the accountant write this letter. See here, it states that the money has been taken and there is no accounting for it. All of it has been since Declan arrived here. He used you to get to your money, and now he's probably off somewhere enjoying it."

"No, you're wrong."

"Then where is he? Where's your truck?"

"He's at a job interview. I told him to use the truck. He'll be back any minute."

Lacey's gaze shot to the door. "Believe what you will. I mean, he'll probably spin this to make himself the good guy. He'll probably say he invested it for you or it wasn't him. It was me. Yeah, that's what he'll do. He'll accuse me of being the thief. Who will you believe then? A person you've known for years, or an ex-con you met a few months ago?"

Lacey didn't give Felicia a chance to respond before she tore out of the house, leaving Felicia gripping the letter in her hands. Hours and hours she sat staring at the letter as the moon rose into the sky. Not because she was looking for Declan's guilt but for the proof he was innocent. *She* knew he was innocent, but she knew she'd need to find the proof for others like the sheriff and Davey.

By midnight, she had looked through all the documents, but she wasn't good with the books. She'd never been great at math, but they looked like what Lacey had said.

Lights flooded through the front window, and the old clock on the wall struck two, as if announcing Declan's return. She froze. She'd waited most of the night to speak to him, and now she couldn't think of anything to say. Lacey was right about one thing. Even if a Supreme Court judge gave her these papers, she wouldn't believe them. If she didn't know Declan like she did and have the feelings she did, she would likely see them the same way.

TWENTY-FOUR

Declan put the truck in park and stretched the kinks of the long day from his neck and back. He hadn't anticipated it taking all day, but the interview had been productive. James had been nothing but kind, and the man wasn't capable of judgement. He hopped out of the truck with a spring in his step, longing to tell Felicia everything, to declare their relationship official, that he'd have a real job, with benefits and income.

A light shone through the front window from the kitchen. Had Felicia waited up for him? A rush of adrenaline filled every nerve ending in his body, so he bolted into the house without even knocking, ready to share the life-altering news.

Felicia sat at the table with a frown, downcast gaze telling him something was wrong. A hundred horrific images of Nana suffering another stroke, the front crop flooded, the business going under all flashed in two blinks.

He raced to her side. "What is it?"

She turned her head and looked at him with a distant gaze, as if she didn't see him.

"You okay? What happened?" He clutched her arms and turned her to face him. "You're scaring me. Please, tell me."

When he didn't get a response, he searched the area for answers. He raced to Nana's room, finding her snoring and well. When he returned, Felicia still sat mute at the table. He knelt by her side and took both her hands in his, placing her palm to his chest. "My heart is beating like a wild bronco. What's wrong? Tell me. You can tell me anything."

"Embezzlement," she breathed more than spoke the one life-altering word.

He fell back onto his heels. "What are you talking about?"

"That's what this letter says." She slid her hand free from his and passed him a piece of paper on formal letterhead from some firm he'd never heard of.

"What's this?" He scanned the words on the paper, accusing someone of stealing money from the nursery. She knew. She'd found out about what Lacey had been doing. He tossed the paper to the side and pulled her into his arms. "I'm so sorry, my dear, sweet Felicia. I'm so sorry."

Her eyes shot wide. "No, it's not true. It can't be."

"I'm sorry I didn't tell you. I know I should have, but I didn't know how. I've fallen for you, and I didn't want to hurt you."

"You didn't want to hurt me?" Felicia shouted. Her words came out like a strangled cry.

"No. I'd never want to hurt you. I...I love you."

"Love me?" Felicia grabbed his shirt with an iron grip. "No, you could never steal from me. Tell me it's not true."

"What?" Fire burned his skin, searing up his spine to the back of his neck. "It wasn't me. I didn't steal from you. I discovered what Lacey was doing, and I confronted her. Did she tell you I was the one stealing?" He attempted to pull her hands free and take her into his arms, but he couldn't unfurl her fingers without worrying about hurting her.

Her hands released him and slipped to her lap. "She said you'd say that." Felicia chuckled, but tears streamed down her face. "Lacey said that's why she went to a forensic accountant." She swiped the tears from her cheeks. "I didn't believe her. The Declan Mills I know wouldn't do such a thing."

"You're right, I wouldn't." He stood and paced around the table, one word echoing in his head. "You said you didn't believe her. As if you do now."

"No, of course not."

Her voice didn't convince him. "But?"

"No buts."

"You don't believe me now."

"It's not that. It's just that I know a man who says he has a mother in a facility in Riverbend, yet I've never met her. Why? Because you've never taken me to meet her."

He shook his head, willing her to understand. "She only agreed to see me that one time. She won't see me again. I didn't want to put you through going and feeling the rejection that I feel every time I try to visit her."

She looked up at him with bloodshot eyes. "Don't you see, it isn't about innocence or guilt. It's about trust. When you took so long to return, I worried you were keeping some other plan to make your life better a secret from me. I believe in you and trust that you wouldn't steal from me, but you've never trusted me with the whole truth about anything."

He wanted to make her see all he'd done was for her. "I did go for a job interview. I'm late because the bridge at the river was flooded and I couldn't get through. I had to drive fifty miles out of the way to get home. Two detours more, and I'm finally here. I did all that to be here with you."

"Yes, you're here now and you declare your love, yet you still keep your distance from me. Do you see how messed up this is? Felicia stood and circled the small living room. "When do you start trusting me with the truth and stop running from us?"

Declan didn't try to catch her or touch her the way his body craved. In that moment, he realized how all this had to look to Felicia. "That's what this is about. You feel rejected."

"Rejected?" Felicia lifted her chin. "No, I feel confused, lost, tired."

His heart sank to his gut. "I knew this would happen. I see it in your eyes. The doubt."

"I told you, this isn't about guilt or innocence. It's about you letting me in. Telling me everything, trusting me with your truth."

He shook his head. "No, I see it in your eyes. You might not believe Lacey, but you don't believe me either. If you won't admit it to me, admit it to yourself. Why did I think there could be a future for me here, with you? I've been lying to myself. There's no way any woman could ever believe a man with a history like mine." He stepped toward the door. His insides shredded with the realization that he'd lost her to his past, like he'd lost everything else. Enough. He wouldn't continue to let everything be taken from him. He wouldn't lose his freedom this time. "I'm not taking the fall this time, though. I'll prove my innocence. I'm just sorry that I had my hopes up about everything between us. I was excited tonight to return and tell you that I got the job."

A sound, almost like a whimper, came from Felicia, but he ignored it. He needed to be strong. This time, he wouldn't allow himself to believe in miracles and happily ever afters. He needed to take care of himself and make sure he stayed out of jail. But one glance at the woman only feet from him, and he knew he'd never be able to allow another woman into his life. She was it. His everything, and she was lost to him.

"Go ahead and run. It's what you do best. Putting distance between us."

Declan stopped dead at the door and faced Felicia one last time. "I won't run. I wouldn't put you through that. All I'm going to say is that I'm innocent. I have no proof yet. But I *am* innocent. I'm warning you now, though. I won't take the fall for someone else again. I will not stop until Lacey is arrested and tried for a crime she tried to pin on me." He bolted out the front door. His stomach roiled and protested the fast food he'd consumed on the way home trying to hurry back to Felicia.

With heavy steps, he stumbled into the camper and sank onto his bed.

His hands shook.

His mind shook.

His heart shook.

Shook with the realization that the woman he loved said she believed him, but she was still letting the accusations against him make her feelings waver. That the one person he thought would never see him as a criminal had just let one piece of paper change the foundation of their relationship.

Stella's father had been right about one thing when he'd dragged him into Sugar Maple searching for his daughter. No one would ever really believe an ex-con.

TWENTY-FIVE

Felicia didn't bother going to bed. She spent the night tossing and turning on the couch. When Nana woke, Felicia rose and fixed breakfast in a fog.

"Dear Lord in heaven, what's wrong with you child?" Nana asked, settling into her seat at the kitchen table.

The rain continued at a ferocious downpour, and she tried to think about the plants, but she couldn't. Her mind could only focus on Declan, Lacey, and the accusations between them.

"What's this?" Nana picked up one of the accusatory documents Lacey had provided.

Felicia broke an egg into the frying pan too forcefully, sending yolk down the side. She grabbed a paper towel and caught the runny yellow before it hit the stovetop. "It's documentation that states Declan stole money from the nursery."

"Hogwash." Nana tossed the paper down. "Who filled your head with such nonsense?"

Felicia stirred the eggs into a runny, unappetizing mess. She didn't want to talk about it, but she knew Nana wouldn't rest until she had more information. "Lacey."

"You going to listen to a using half-wit addicted to a bad

man, or Declan, the one who's been busting his butt to help you these last couple of months?"

"Nana, it's there. In front of you. Who wouldn't believe it?" She sighed. "But no, I don't believe it. I don't know what's going on, but I know he wouldn't steal from us. Yet, he's not the man I thought he was. I made him into a man that would be an answer to all my prayers. A gift to me and you. A lie covered in hope."

"Hogwash."

"Stop saying that. You don't understand. I told him I didn't believe it, but he ran off anyway. That's all Declan knows how to do. He lets me in and then pushes me away over and over again, and I'm tired of it."

Nana beat her cane against the floor twice. "This isn't evidence. It's a tool to drive that man out of town, and you're letting it work. That girl's been threatened by Declan since he arrived. You put him in her job and set them against each other from day one. She has no home and is mixed up with all sorts of crazy. Don't let her destroy what you have with Declan."

"What do I really have with him? A man who turns me around, upside down, and inside out all the time?"

"That's love, you fool," Nana growled.

Felicia slid the eggs onto a plate, grabbed a fork, and placed it in front of Nana.

"You better put on your raincoat and go to the front field right now." Nana huffed and pushed from the chair.

The smell of eggs stirred Felicia's nausea, so she didn't bother making any more. "Why would I do that?"

Nana used her cane to reach the wall before she turned to face her. "Because you just confirmed Declan's worst fear in life. That no one will ever believe him again."

"I told him I believed him, but he left anyway."

"Are you surprised? I mean, think about it. How many times would it have to happen of people turning their back on you, calling you names, judging you until it would take more than words to convince you otherwise? Would you open your heart completely to someone if you thought they'd only turn their back on you? His own mother turned away from him. Why would you stay at the first sign of trouble?"

Felicia closed her eyes and thought back over all the times he'd shown how much he cared, only to pull away. She hadn't chased him because she thought he'd needed space. In retrospect, had that been the wrong decision? "What do I do to make him trust me, then?"

"You can start by going after him. He's been up at that front field since before daybreak, digging a trench to save your plants. The man's always looking out for you and me. It's not an act. He cares and doesn't want to hurt you. Even if you hurt him."

Deep down, Felicia believed that. Not for one second had she really believed he could steal from her, but she had hesitated when he'd asked her. She'd been protecting her own heart. "What if he decides to leave anyway? He's got a job opportunity and a future away from here."

"You think a job would take him from you?"

Felicia shrugged. "I never thought my parents would leave, and they did."

"Honey, that man is nothing like your parents. He's here to stay. Your father gave up the fight for respect in this town for greener pastures. A life beyond his humble beginnings. That man out there is far stronger than your parents ever were." Nana hobbled a few more steps and stopped. "By the way, Declan came to me for advice a week ago. He tried to play off a hypothetical, but I deduced that he'd confronted Lacey about taking money. When I interrogated him, he caved and told me that a message had popped up on the computer in the office when he was filling out job applications. It was a stream of messages about taking money from you. When Declan confronted her, she vowed she'd take him down and that no one would believe him over her. I guess she was right."

"See?" Felicia threw up her hands in exasperation. "That's the problem. He trusted you with that information, not me."

Nana pushed from the wall and hobbled toward her room. "Maybe you should both stop protecting your hearts and open up to each other. You've always been a good negotiator. Go negotiate. That's one of the things Declan loves about you. That, and you're hot, apparently." She moved her cane ahead and took two steps. "Go make nice with that man, or you're going to starve me to death. Petunia wouldn't eat that slop you cooked."

Felicia eyed the downpour outside, certain Declan wasn't out in it. Then she sighed. Of course he was. The man had done anything and everything to help her since he'd arrived. What a fool she'd been. If she wanted Declan to open up to her, she needed to pry that door ajar.

Felicia grabbed her raincoat and opened the front door to a heavy wind sweeping through the front fields. The water was pouring from the sky so thick she couldn't see twenty feet ahead. She snugged her hood over her head, cinched the collar around her neck, and then, hoping Nana was wrong, raced for the trailer. A streak of lightning lit the sky, and a rumble of thunder shook the ground beneath her. She pounded on the camper door. "Declan, please let me inside!"

Nothing, not even a shadow appeared through the window. Nana had been right. He was out in this weather, working to save her plants with no regard to his safety. She trudged through the soggy grass, into a muddy swamp, before reaching the gravel drive. A figure loomed in the distance, hunched over. She quickened her pace, the rocks cutting into her sock-covered feet. She'd been in such a rush, she'd forgotten her shoes. "Declan! Declan!"

The storm blew leaves from the bent-over trees, bowing to the furious wind. She reached the edge of the field, and it was him. Declan, shoveling mud over his shoulder into the ditch outside the fence.

"What are you doing? It's too dangerous to be out here."

He didn't say anything or even look at her. Instead, he continued to work, taking chunks of earth and flinging it behind him.

"I know you must be mad at me. *I'm* mad at me. You're innocent. It doesn't matter what those papers say."

He impaled the mud with the shovel and flung his hair back to show his piercing eyes in the darkness. "You may think you believe me, but I saw it, your hesitation. And you had every right to doubt me. I'm a man who's on probation. You deserve better than that."

"Stop. Just stop pushing me away. Yes, I hesitated, not because I believed Lacey but because I've been scared, and it was easier to push you away than to keep having you play with my emotions." She stepped forward, her feet slurping with each step. "Give me a chance and open your heart to me. You've done so much for me since you've arrived, more than any person has ever done, next to my grandmother, and I blew it. I should've taken a chance and forced you to see how much you mean to me instead of protecting myself from rejection. There's nothing I can do about your record from before, but I can prove your innocence this time. I promise to clear your name and prove you weren't the one who stole money from the nursery. I'll even send Lacey to jail. Please, tell me what I can do to make this right between us. Tell me what I can do to prove how I feel about you. How I trust you. How I love you."

He turned from her and clutched the handle of the shovel. "It's no use. Lacey's going to turn me into the police along with those documents, and there's nothing I can do to fight back. No one will listen to an ex-con."

Felicia grabbed hold of his sleeve, which was drenched in sweat and rain. "I will. I'll listen. More than that. We'll fight this together. There has to be some way to show this is all lies. And you're the man to help me prove it. Say you'll do it. Help me clear your name and prove to the world once and for all that you're the amazing, smart, charismatic, honest, loving gift from God that you are."

His jaw twitched, his gaze searched the massive hole he'd made leading out to the ditch, and then he searched her face, leaving her feeling vulnerable, breathless, hopeful. "No." He yanked the shovel from the ground and stared her down. "I won't prove who I am to the world."

She grabbed hold of his shirt, popping several buttons. "You have to."

"I won't waste my time proving myself to the world, but I'll prove myself worthy of your love."

TWENTY-SIX

Water dripped from Declan's hair, sending muddy raindrops into his mouth. He'd tasted that flavor on more than one occasion when he'd first entered the system. The new guy tasted dirt in the yard on a regular basis. He'd learned how to survive then, and he'd learn how to survive now. He stormed past Felicia, up the gravel drive, and shoved the door open to the office, hoping she'd follow him out of the rain. The last thing she needed was to get sick.

It didn't matter how much she professed her belief in Declan. He couldn't let it go. No way would he start a life with someone who had any doubts of his innocence. "It doesn't matter what you think now. What happens when someone more credible accuses me of a crime? I don't know that we have a future together, but if we do, we need to work through this first. Otherwise, a police officer could show up at any moment and arrest me."

Felicia opened a drawer and snagged a towel out of it, wiping her face and then tossing it to him. "I won't let that happen."

"You can't stop it," he grumbled, wiping his face and arms free of sludge.

Her hand covered the towel, stopping him midswipe. She took the cloth from him and dabbed at his neck and cheeks. "Help me, then."

"How?" A shiver went through her, so he pulled her to his chest and held her tight. The warmth of her body heated him from the inside out.

They stood in the middle of the office, breathing in unison, clinging to one another and the hope of possibilities. She leaned back, slipping her fingers under the hem of his shirt. She tugged it up, and he leaned down so she could slip it over his head. She pressed the towel to his chest, soaking up each drop before she moved lower to his stomach.

He sucked in a quick breath and stayed her hands. "Stop." With every ounce of his waning determination, he managed to step away, turning to face the outside world, and clutch the wood beam on the wall. He squeezed tight to hold on to something in order to keep his hands off the woman he wanted more than his next breath. "I won't allow myself to be with you when I could be gone tomorrow. It would kill me to know I lost you. I won't survive another year behind bars. Not after I've tasted the freedom of working outside, breathing fresh air...of you." His knuckles popped under the pressure of his grip.

For several moments, all he heard was the wind and rain outside until he finally spoke again. "I'm sorry. I can't. I just can't have a life again only to lose it."

Her arms slipped around him from behind. "Then let's make sure you don't lose it." Her short nails traced around his belly button, drawing his breath. "Help me go through the documents, through the computer, until we discover our own evidence. If you need this to finally let yourself believe in us, then let's figure it out."

"There isn't time. You and I both know that Lacey won't stop. The police will be here before we even have a chance to comb through all those documents."

"I'll tell Lacey that I'm going to report you but not until the show's over. That I need your help until then. That'll buy us some time," Felicia whispered into his back, pressing a kiss to his spine that seared through his skin, his lungs, all the way to his soul.

That was it. He couldn't hold back any longer. He turned, but she had slipped away.

"No. I know that look, but you can't. The next time you kiss me like that, it isn't going to be a hit and run." Felicia's lip quivered. She backed away to the threshold. "Get cleaned up and then we can meet back here in a bit. I need you to trust me."

"God help me, I do." He ran his hand through his hair. The cold of the damp air and the heat of his desire for Felicia made him tremble, but she was right. Passion wasn't the answer, not now. Did he dare believe there would be a right moment for them? A real moment without his past looming over them, threat of jail around them, and darkness ahead of them?

He didn't know, but he knew he had to keep fighting or he'd lose everything. "I'll meet you back here in twenty minutes."

Without taking time to think, he showered, dressed, and returned to the office. Thank goodness the rain had finally calmed to a slight drizzle. Unfortunately, when he sat waiting for Felicia to return, his brain went into gear. This plan could work against him. Last time he tried to figure out how someone was stealing money, he found himself confessing to the crime.

Felicia entered with papers in hand and opened the laptop. "Let's get started."

"It feels like we're tempting fate," he mumbled under his breath.

"I don't believe in fate. I believe in working hard and creating the life you want."

He raised a brow at her. "So you don't believe fate brought us together? I thought all girls believed in that stuff."

"Nope. You brought yourself here believing you were helping people. Now, you're going to help yourself." Felicia opened the computer and brought up banking statements and spreadsheets. "This is where I need your help. I've never been good with numbers. My grandmother handled all the accounting until her stroke a little over a year ago."

"That means any criminal activity happened in the last twelve months." He eyed the computer. "How long has Jason been controlling Lacey?"

Felicia rolled a pencil under her hand and pressed her lips together before she spoke again. "I'd say a couple of months before you arrived."

"Great. That narrows it down. Let me see those documents."

Felicia pushed them in front of him. "If she wanted you to take the fall, that narrows it down even further to the last couple of months."

"Not necessarily. I think they started taking money before I arrived but didn't bother covering their tracks until I intercepted that note. They had to have worked quickly, too." He switched back to the computer. "Wait. The spreadsheets on the computer are shared with Lacey, right? She has access to them?"

"Yes, the file is shared through the drive." Felicia hovered over his shoulder.

"Perfect." He went to File and selected File History. "The changes are shown here. We'll have to compare this to the sheets she has printed. I know there'll be evidence in here."

He scanned the right column with the list of changes, and his gut clenched tight. "It won't work."

Felicia settled in next to him. "Why?"

He fisted his hand and slammed it to the desk, making everything vibrate. "Because she's smarter than I thought." He pointed at the screen. "See this? She reverted to the version from four months ago and then made all the changes she wished to match to the current sheet. If she's smart enough to do that, then she's smart enough to cover her tracks when recreating it. See here, the discrepancies entered are all since I arrived."

Felicia smiled, a blooming of mischief kind of smile.

"What?" He narrowed his gaze at her. "This isn't good."

"Because." She got up, unlocked a cabinet drawer, and pulled out two large folders. "Lacey doesn't know that I print everything off each month and store a hard copy. I didn't do it because I was suspicious but because I keep trying to get my grandmother to look over things for me so that she'll feel important again. I should've known Nana would save the day."

TWENTY-SEVEN

Felicia's cell rang. She didn't have to look at the number to know it was Lacey. The girl had been texting her since yesterday, and when she called to tell Lacey there was news, it didn't take her thirty seconds to answer.

"Hello? Is everything okay?"

"Yes, Lacey. I've made a decision."

"What?"

Muffled grumbling in the background of a man in a rage told Felicia things were no better with Jason. "Are you okay?"

"Yeah, why wouldn't I be? It's you that I'm worried about with that man stealing from you all the time. What are you going to do?"

She wanted to press further, tell Lacey to come home and leave that man behind, but it wouldn't do any good. Lacey had left them no choice but to move forward with their plan. "Two days. After the filming at the nursery, I'm going to have the police come and arrest Declan." Felicia had to force the bitter words from her mouth, despite her stomach's protest.

"Why then? Do it now."

"Lacey, I need him for the shoot. There's no one else who

can handle the heavy lifting, and there's no time to find some-one." Felicia had practiced her response and looked to Declan for his nod of approval.

"Jason." Lacey sucked in a breath like a whistle through the phone. "Yeah, he needs work and so do I. We'll come over tomorrow, and we'll have him arrested, and then we'll get to work helping you."

Felicia spun in all directions, looking for answers on the couch, wall clock, television, and then settled on Declan. "No. You and I both know he is the man for the job. Not even the three of us can manage the work load he does on his own. Once this filming is over, I can put an advertisement out for someone strong and able bodied like him, but there isn't time right now."

Declan waved his arms, clearly warning her not to go off script.

"No. I gave you what you need." Lacey's voice cracked, and the sound of something slamming echoed through the phone.

Felicia had to stifle her need to beg Lacey to get away from Jason. Despite everything, she didn't like what Lacey was going through, but the girl had made her choice when she framed Declan.

Felicia forced a calm, coldness to her voice she didn't feel. "Yes, and I'm going to use it to put Declan away for a long time."

"Fine," Lacey said in a defeated tone.

Someone covered the receiver. For several long seconds, all Felicia could hear was a deep voice, but no words came through clear. The ruffle of a hand over the phone uncovered, and Lacey said, "We'll help. We'll be there for the shoot to make sure everything goes as planned. You can't do it alone."

"Thanks. It's nice to know after everything, you still have my back, Lacey."

The phone clicked, ending the call.

Felicia collapsed onto the couch next to Declan and held her head in her hands. "I panicked."

Declan rubbed soothing circles on her back. "Do you think she was on to you?"

She shrugged but then let out a long sigh and said, "I don't think so. I mean, it played out like you said. They want to be here for the big event."

"It gives us two days to get our side of the story put together, and it's the only way we'll be able to get them here and turn everything over to the police," Declan said in an I've-got-your-back tone. "If they get wind of what we're doing and they have time to react, I don't know what they'll do. I worry for your safety."

"Do we have anything to turn over?" Felicia dared a glance to see his brows furrowed and that vibration under his right eye that always appeared when he was stressed.

"Under normal circumstances, yes, but we both have documentation."

"That's enough to clear you, right?"

"I have a record. Lacey doesn't. She's a local. I'm not. Even if I was given the opportunity to speak, it would be a long and drawn-out process. I honestly don't know if I'd be put in jail because my parole officer decides I'm a flight risk and my probation is revoked. I mean, think about it. This is exactly what I served time for in the first place. It doesn't look good."

"But I'll tell the truth," Felicia insisted. "Besides, if I don't press charges, they can't go after you."

"Based on my experience, they can do what they want if they believe you're guilty. Sure, they might not be able to convict me, but they can punish me with jail time nonetheless."

"That isn't fair!" Felicia pushed from the couch, walked to the table, and searched the dozens of papers they'd been through so many times. "Fine, then I'll lie and tell them that I saw Lacey stealing and that I know it was her."

Declan took both her hands and drew her onto his lap, brushing her hair from her eyes and lifting her chin to look at him. "I want you to hear me now, Felicia Hughes. You're the most pure person I know. You help everyone. I never want you to have to lie for me or anyone else. No more. I won't be the cause of you discovering a darker side to doing things like Jason has taught Lacey."

"It's not the same thing," Felicia snapped.

He pressed a kiss to her cheek and whispered, "It's exactly the same thing."

She wanted to argue with him, but she hadn't felt good moments earlier on the phone with Lacey. Nothing about this felt right, but she wanted to save Declan. "Then what do we do?"

"I tell you what you sniffling fools do." Nana shoved her cane forward and took two steps into the room. "You win. I didn't raise no loser."

Declan chuckled. "If we're going to win, we need all hands on spreadsheets. You willing to try to keep me here with you and Felicia?"

"Bring me my glasses." Nana shuffled forward, and Declan was at her side, helping her into the dining chair. "We've got work to do."

TWENTY-EIGHT

The sight of the film crew's arrival jump-started Declan's nerves. There'd be too many variables, and they only had circumstantial evidence against Lacey. Despite the definitive proof that someone had changed the spreadsheets from what it was months ago, they couldn't show who'd made those changes.

Men set up a tent out on the front open field, and equipment was offloaded from the vans. He took in a deep breath and prepared himself for today. He'd texted James that he'd start his new job in a week, allowing him to work out all these issue prior to starting. Everything was in his reach, including Felicia. Now he just needed to hold out a little longer.

Two hands slid over his shoulders, and his body responded, telling him it was Felicia. Her touch was like a promise of a rainbow in a dark storm. The light beyond the three white walls of a cell to guide him to freedom. His hope never to return to the loneliness of an empty cell overwhelmed him. Solitary life was like a manic unable to find stimulus—harsh, isolating, inhuman.

"Everything will be great. As soon as she arrives, I'll turn her and the evidence, along with my written statement, over to the police."

"Don't forget mine. I'm in this too you know." Nana waved her cane. The woman had made such progress since he'd arrived. Was Felicia right? Had he been part of the motivation to get her out of her room and back to life again? "And don't go thinking they'll dismiss me because I'm an angry old bat. I'm an elder, and what I say matters. Already spoke to Ms. Melba and Ms. Gina. Davey's on the fence, but we'll get him to cross over to Declan's side."

Felicia took him by the hand and led him to the front door. She paused, blocking their exit. "Listen, no matter what, I'm going to fight for you. That being said, if you decide that this isn't the life you want, that you want to move on without me, you have my blessing. The next time you kiss me, it's going to be one that starts our lives together, so make sure before you take me into your arms that you mean it. If not, then go to Creekside and make a life for yourself. You deserve it."

He opened his mouth to tell her how he felt, but she put a finger to his lips. "Wait. Once you're free of this drama, you might see things differently. Don't make a promise to me now that you don't keep later." She withdrew from him, opened the door, and strutted out to the center of her friend group, leaving him on the outskirts to watch.

He was tired of being on the sidelines. He wanted to be in the middle of Felicia's life.

The grass squished and water gushed from under his work boots, but the puddles had dried up. It wasn't long before he was whisked into action, moving plants, props, and filming paraphernalia. The activity calmed his anxiety, and the familiar joy of a hard day of labor eked into his consciousness. He'd never been this happy working behind a desk. Perhaps he would enjoy the job at the VA more since it wasn't all sitting and paperwork.

Knox Brevard directed Felicia to her spot. His hand on her back sent a hint of jealousy through Declan, despite the knowledge he was all about Stella. He'd never been that kind of man before, but he'd never met a woman like Felicia. His father had once told him that he knew Declan's mother was the right one after five minutes, but it took him five months to admit it to himself. That had never made any sense to Declan, until now.

Stella and the other girls hovered nearby, watching the filming, him, and the driveway. They were in on it. Felicia wouldn't have it any other way. The Fabulous Five were here and, from what he understood, a power like no other in town.

"Action." The word echoed from the front field where they'd managed to save the plants during the storm. Most of them anyway.

Felicia spoke in a fast clip with a high pitch to her voice for several sentences, but Knox directed her attention to a flower and she lit up, settling into her normal, enigmatic personality that Declan knew everyone would love. This nursery would be bursting with customers soon. The land behind them would have to be purchased to allow for more growth. They could sell fruits, vegetables, and herbs seasonally, along with an online floral club. Fresh-cut flowers delivered to your door monthly. The possibilities were popping up like weeds in his brain—damaging, distracting, and dangerous to life around them.

This wasn't his land or his business. He needed to find his own way, not live off her. Felicia deserved far better than him. And despite that knowledge, he couldn't let her go. He'd have to make this work, or he'd go to jail trying.

A rusted, olive green beater he knew to be Jason's car pulled into the driveway and maneuvered around the production vehicles to park at the hog wire fence at the front of the property near the sheriff's car. His pulse quickened, and his gaze darted to the four women huddled around Drew Lancaster, Mayor Horton, and her fiancé, Mr. Strickland. He swallowed the hewn pole–sized lump in his throat and forced his attention to the filming.

The film crew broke down the set in the front field and moved to the orchard to set up for the next shot. A streak of black across the side yard drew his attention. Someone ran between the vehicles but disappeared beyond the other side of the house.

"Enjoying the show?" Lacey's voice came with venom and hate. How did one young woman have so much pain inside her? He wasn't sure if he wanted to yell at her or pull her into his arms and promise to run Jason out of her life.

He cleared his throat. "What are you doing here?" Of course, he knew she was here to witness his demise and arrest, but he couldn't slip or he'd give her an opportunity to come up with some other devious plan.

"I was invited. You know, I'm a member of this town," she said with an I'm-here-to-put-you-in-your-place tone.

The sheriff strutted across the field toward the vehicles, telling Declan he'd seen the figure that had moved in the distance also. Good. He was on it, letting Declan relax a little.

He forced the words he wanted to say into submission and lifted his chin. "Excuse me. I need to get back to work." In an attempt to look busy, he went to the front field, where they'd finished filming, and fixed some of the damaged damp earth near the roots of several flowers, picked up a few pieces of trash, and then threw them away at the garbage can under the main tent.

Stella sidled up next to him. "It's going to be fine. We've got Felicia's back."

"Thank you for that. I'm glad she has such amazing friends in her life."

"That means we have your back." Stella put a hand on her hip and did her hip out, ponytail flip thing, yet her face was soft.

"Gotta make Lacey believe I'm not, though. I never liked that girl. Told Felicia to get rid of her, but she can never turn away a stray."

"Ouch." He looked over Stella's head and noticed Lacey slip away to the side of the house.

Mary-Beth slid her hand into the crook of Stella's arm, which made the girl flinch. "Don't listen to her. Some strays are better than purebreds. They're loving and loyal instead of snotty and self-serving."

Stella stiffened and snarled down at Mary-Beth's touch before she regained her composure. "I was just initiating the new guy, since it appears he'll be staying around our sweet girl." She marched off to the orchard with a half-smile at Knox Brevard who was waving her over.

With everyone's attention on the filming, and the sheriff off looking for the person Declan believed to be Jason stalking around the property, Declan decided to check and see what Lacey was up to. No way he'd let her do any more damage. Why the sheriff hadn't just come and arrested her when she arrived, he wasn't sure, but Sugar Maple had a plan, and who was he to question it. Felicia had told him not to worry, that they only wanted to get through the filming before the drama happened, but he didn't like it. Not one bit.

At the edge of the house, he noticed the office door cracked, and he knew Lacey was inside, probably making sure to seal his fate. Without another thought, he barged into the office and discovered her prying open the filing cabinet. "You won't find anything in there."

She grasped the cutting shears in her hand and held them up to him.

"You can try, but I assure you, you better make it a good stab because you'll only get one shot at it."

She looked down at her hand, and her mouth fell open.

That's when he saw them, the rings around her blood shot eyes. How had he missed them? "You poor thing. That man has you strung out."

"You don't know what you're talking about." She tossed the sharp shears onto the desk and made for the door but stopped short.

"What's he doing in here?" Jason's voice echoed into the small office from behind Declan. "Go get the sheriff. It's time we end this."

Lacey didn't move.

"Did you hear me? Are you that stupid? Move it."

"Don't call her stupid, you worthless excuse for a man." Declan's hackles rose, his anger bubbling to the surface.

Jason stumbled back a step. "You better not touch me. I'll get you for assault, too." He lifted his boney chin high. "Better yet, go ahead. More jail time for you." He glowered at Lacey. "Did you get it done?"

She shook her head vigorously with wide eyes.

"You're so incompetent. I can't trust you to do anything. I told you there would be hard copies, but you were too stupid to get them."

"Don't talk to her that way." Declan shot forward, but Lacey jumped between them.

"Don't hurt him," Lacey screeched.

"Are you still protecting him?" Declan softened his expression and muscles in hopes of calming Lacey enough to listen. "You're a beautiful, competent young woman with people who care about you. Don't you see that you deserve better? Do you want to fall into a pit of drugs and unhappiness?"

"Unhappiness?" Tears filled her eyes, and he knew he'd hit a nerve.

"Yes. Think back. When were you last truly happy?"

Declan willed her to listen but wasn't hopeful that she'd hear his words.

"I...I don't know." Lacey studied the floor.

"Happiness is a myth. It doesn't exist. Parents leave. Employers can you. Women are all drama." Jason backed to the threshold. "Let's go. I take care of you. No one else will. Your mother and Felicia turned their backs on you."

"No, they didn't. Even now, Felicia would welcome you back."

Her gaze shot to him. "She would?"

The weeks of abuse, exhaustion, and hitting life's bottom showed like a flashing billboard on her face. At that moment, he didn't hate Lacey or wish to punish her. He only wanted her to be okay. "Absolutely. And your job is available again, too. I'm leaving for a job in Creekside."

"You are?"

"Don't listen to him. He'll say anything to keep himself out of jail," Jason shouted.

Her gaze snapped to him, and Declan worried he'd lost her.

"Who would hire an ex-con? Jason says there're no other jobs for people like you."

Declan wanted to shake her until she saw the truth, but that tactic was more Jason's style. "A man who works at a VA center in Creekside believes in second chances. That's his job, getting veterans back on their feet. It isn't a job like I had before. I'll be doing transportation, paperwork, intake stuff, and some book work. I'm supposed to start next week." He dared to step closer, brushing her arm up and down as if soothing a wild animal, and kept his gaze trained on her, ignoring the other man even as he sensed Jason moving away. "I'll even be moving my camper close to Creekside."

Voices sounded in the distance but drew closer.

"Let's go. Now," Jason ordered.

"Wait," Lacey said in a little-girl-in-trouble tone.

"No more waiting," Jason ordered.

A flash of light drew Declan's attention, and he saw Jason outside holding a bottle with an inflamed rag hanging from it. "Good-bye."

Declan shot forward. The bottle flew past his shoulder too fast to grab it. It smashed to the floor, erupting in smoke-inducing orange and yellow light.

Jason shot back. "Get me or save Lacey."

He took off, and Declan didn't have time to chase him, not when the ravenous fire gobbled up the wood walls and desk.

He grabbed Lacey. "Come on. We need to get out of here." Smoke filled the room, so he felt for her hand until he had hold of her and then dragged her from the burning room. The flames licked at the outside and climbed the walls to the roof. "Help! Fire!"

People rushed over, cell phones in hand, reporting to emergency services.

He ushered Lacey away from the fire to the safety of the front yard. Felicia raced to their side, her four friends and the town behind her. Declan eyed the flames stretching toward the sky and catching the shingles on the roof of the house.

"Nana," he breathed.

His feet moved before his brain could even process the danger. He shot across the front yard and into the house, which was already filling with smoke. "Nana!"

TWENTY-NINE

Fire engine sirens blared in the distance. Felicia shoved and pushed, but Knox wouldn't release her.

"Stop. There's nothing you can do," he said with a soft but firm voice.

Drew Lancaster tried to get close, but the flames enveloped the front of the house quicker than anyone could have imagined. Her home and her family were being destroyed in front of her eyes.

Stella moved, blocking Felicia's view of the inferno. "Listen, the fire department's almost here."

Sirens were barely audible through the pounding in Felicia's ears. "Dear Lord in heaven, please help," she begged aloud. She struggled again, but there was no getting away from Knox. Even if she did, her friends formed a human shield between her and danger.

"Declan!" she screamed, tears streaming down her face.

The fire engine pulled onto the gravel road but couldn't get through.

Stella rushed into action. "Move your cars!"

Everyone darted to their vehicles, but they only caused a

traffic jam, bottlenecking cars trying to escape through the gate. Stella hopped in her Chevy and rammed the fence Declan had spent weeks repairing, giving more space for the cars to move.

A firefighter with an axe mowed through the crowd. "Move away from the house."

Knox dragged Felicia back, leaving two lines from her boots in the mud. Drew shouted something from the side of the house, and the firefighter followed him to the back, beyond their field of vision.

Breath caught in her lungs and couldn't escape. There was a burning, itching pressure in her chest, as if she were the one trapped inside her burning home.

"Someone move the camper away from the house," another firefighter ordered.

Mary-Beth looked to Felicia.

She shook her head, dislodging the haze. "Keys are inside the camper."

Mary-Beth took off with the firefighter at her side.

The peaceful world of her once beautiful home and nursery erupted in a fury of people trudging through flowers, busting windows, and the odor of burning wood. At the sight of the flames engulfing the front of the home, her body went numb and she collapsed. Knox lowered her to the ground, and Carissa held tight to her. At that moment, Felicia realized not only were her grandmother and the man she loved inside, but Carissa waited to discover Drew's fate, too.

Lacey hovered nearby, rocking, biting her nails. "I'm so sorry. I didn't know."

Felicia shot her a narrow-eyed look that told Lacey she'd never be welcome in her life again.

A crash, the breaking of glass, sounded again, and there were shouts coming from the other side of the blaze.

"We got her!" The words were like a day lily opening to the

morning sun for the first time. But as a labored breath entered, so did the realization they said her. Not them.

Carissa squeezed her tight into her side, pleading almost under her breath, "Drew. Come on. You can't leave me now!"

A figure broke through the smoke. The helmet said firefighter, and he carried Nana in his arms. Felicia was elated and devastated all at the same time. "Where are the men? Where are Declan and Drew?"

She shot from Carissa to the gurney, where the fireman set her grandmother. "Where are the others?"

"I don't know, ma'am. I was passed this woman and brought her for treatment."

Nana coughed and gasped, fighting the mask being shoved onto her face.

"Ma'am, we need you to relax," the paramedic told her, but she wouldn't, so Felicia took her hand.

"It's okay. Let them do their job. I'm here."

"Inside the window. He passed me out. Declan's just inside the window," Nana rasped.

Felicia took off, but someone grabbed hold, wrapping their strong arms around her waist. "Help him! He's just inside the window where he passed my grandmother out. Someone do something!"

The water from the fire hose beating against the roof caused more smoke to plume, but another male figure exited the smoke. Her heart raced. She blinked through the stinging in her eyes, but when Carissa rushed past and launched into his arms, she knew it was Drew.

"Where is he? Where's Declan?" Felicia cried out, begging for information.

Drew coughed and clung to Carissa, plastering her face with sweet kisses. "He went inside, but he didn't come out yet."

Carissa held him up the best she could, but one of the firemen took him and helped him to the ambulance.

Felicia felt the life drain from inside her. The world was as dark as the black smoke rising before her. She heaved in a stuttered breath, but she wouldn't give up, not yet. She would never give up on Declan Mills. "Please, someone help him."

"It's okay. We're here." Jackie took her hand, Stella at her side. The strong arms from around her middle released, and both girls held her tight.

Ms. Horton took her hands. "I'm here, dear girl. We're all here."

"All clear," someone yelled.

"No. Declan's still inside." Felicia tried to move, but the women all held tight. "He's not out! Someone help him!"

Three men rounded the corner and removed their helmets. The front man took in a deep breath and faced her. "We're doing all we can, ma'am, but the house is going to suffer extensive damage. Do you have somewhere to stay?"

"Yes, she always has a place to stay," Ms. Horton announced. "She can always stay with me."

"Or in my camper," a raspy voice managed to say between coughs.

It wasn't just any voice. It was Declan's that broke through the barrier of pain and anguish and the two men between them. His face was covered in gray, the edges of his shirt singed, his hair disheveled, but it was him.

She lunged into his arms and held tight, tighter than she'd ever held to anyone or anything in her life. "Don't ever leave me like that again," she sobbed. Tears flowed, her body shook, but her heart warmed at the feel of him against her.

THIRTY

Declan and Felicia stood side-by-side watching the burning embers being doused. The ambulance transporting Nana and Ms. Horton, who'd offered to accompany Felicia's grandmother to the hospital, rolled off the driveway and onto the main road. He knew Felicia wanted to go, but Nana was only getting checked out as a precaution, and the sheriff had asked Felicia to stay.

Now that the flames were under control, the sheriff approached with a determined expression. "Felicia, I received information that this fire was started by someone and that it was intentional."

Declan nodded. "Your information is correct, Sheriff."

The man pressed his lips together and removed his cuffs. "I'm sorry to hear that. Please turn around for me."

"Wait, what?" Felicia shot in front of him as if a protective shield.

"No. I didn't do this. I'd never harm Felicia or her grandmother," Declan protested. "Jason did."

"According to Jason, he witnessed you start the fire to cover evidence of stealing money from Ms. Hughes."

"It wasn't him. It was Jason and Lacey. Arrest her." Felicia pointed to the young woman, her cousin and once dear friend.

"No. Don't." Declan sighed. "She didn't start the fire, either. It was Jason alone. He's been influencing Lacey with mental games, drugs, and lies. She's confused and disoriented, and she needs help, not jail."

Lacey stood with a blank stare, as if unable to process anything.

Felicia rounded on her. "Tell the truth. For once, stop being selfish, stop being manipulated, and stop lying. You're about to send an innocent man to jail."

"Jason said Declan was harming you. That he needs to be taken away if I wanted to help you," Lacey mumbled as if in a trance.

Declan took Felicia's hand and kissed her knuckles. "Don't be mad at her. She needs your love now more than anything. The woman I know would never hate someone. She would only offer help. I learned that from you, that not everyone is going to condemn me, and everyone needs a helping hand at times."

The sheriff cleared his throat. "You need to come with me."

Declan's hands shook. He wanted to run far away, but one glance at Felicia, and he knew he could never run from his feelings for her. "It's okay. I'll go. I believe this will work out."

Felicia clung to him. "No, I won't let you take the fall for this." She faced the sheriff. "I told you that I have proof that Lacey was stealing from me and trying to frame Declan."

"Bring that evidence with you, and we can all go to the station," the sheriff said a little less forcefully.

Declan eyed the half-burned-out home. "She can't. The proof was destroyed in the fire."

"That's unfortunate." The sheriff removed his hat, wiped his brow, and placed it back on his head. He eyed Declan but without narrowed eyes and with a soft stance. "Ms. Lacey Peters. I urge you to work out something with Felicia Hughes in regards to repayment if you were indeed the one to borrow money from her. As for the fire, if all of your statements name this Jason fella as the arsonist, then none of you need to report to the station except to sign official statements. However..." His voice switched to a commanding tone. "If you continue to state that Declan was the one who committed these crimes and later you're discovered to be giving false testimony, you will be facing extensive jail time yourself."

Declan wasn't sure if that was technically correct, but he liked the way the sheriff's words caused Lacey to snap out of whatever daze she was in.

"I...I might have borrowed a few dollars. But I had nothing to do with the fire." She choked and sobbed for a moment, eyeing the home. "I'd never do that to you or Nana." Her pleading gaze focused on Felicia. "I'm so sorry." She broke down, her head in her hands, crying and wailing.

"Do you wish to press charges, Ms. Hughes?"

"Yes, I do."

Lacey stopped her tears and stood straight, frozen.

Declan laced his fingers between Felicia's. "I know you. You'll never be able to live with yourself if you send Lacey to jail. She's the most lost stray you've ever found. And she needs our help."

Felicia smiled. "And that's why I love you, Declan Mills. You understand and support me like no other person. Of course, you'll have to help me explain this to the girls." She looked at the sheriff. "I want to press charges against Jason."

Lacey fell into Felicia's arms. "Please forgive me. I don't know why I did what I did. I was so lost and alone and confused. I promise to make this right. I don't know how, but I will. I'll rebuild your house brick by brick if I have to."

Felicia stroked her hair. "Shh. Don't worry about that now. We'll figure this out together. You, me, Nana, and Declan."

Lacey nodded, but she didn't look up.

The sheriff tipped his hat. "I'll need you to come down to the station later to sign the statement. In the meantime, let the town know what you need."

"You can give Lacey a ride to her mother's house. She doesn't just need to apologize to me. Her mother needs to see her daughter to see she's okay," Felicia said in a firm tone.

Declan was proud of her strength yet compassion for Lacey.

Lacey shot back and shook her head. "No. She hates me. I can't."

"She's your mother and she loves you. Besides, you can't stay here. I'll be staying in a small camper near Creekside for a while until we can rebuild."

"No," Declan said.

Felicia turned to face him, her eyes wide and frown firmly planted on her face. "But..."

"We'll be staying right here. I'm turning the job down. We need to rebuild."

"You don't have to—"

Declan tugged Felicia into his arms. "I want to. I never wanted to leave this place to work anyway. You were right. I belong here. I belong here with you." He kissed her with all the love, passion, and desire he could show her. Life had changed from hopeless, lost, unforgiving, and judged to exciting and full of possibilities. He wanted her to know that he did and always would cherish her.

EPILOGUE

All the residents of Sugar Maple joined in the summer festival. The town square flooded with people, vendors selling their goods and people dancing in the heart of the town under the setting sun.

Declan scanned the town square, spotting the Friendly Five who'd fast accepted him. Stella and Knox who were hanging out with Carissa and Drew. Mary-Beth who sat next to a fireman on a bench. They'd been talking since the day of the fire, but according to Felicia nothing would ever come of it. Not when Mary-Beth still clung to her high school sweetheart that had broken her heart after high school.

A customer tore him from his musings, so he greeted her and showed her several options.

Nana, who'd passed along through Ms. Horton that she had good news to share, walked up on Davey's arm with her cane.

Declan handed the customer her potted floral arrangement that he'd created himself and turned his attention to Nana, with a happy, bright-eyed expression. "Well, good evening, you two. I hear that the house will be done in two weeks, so we'll get to be a family again."

Nana tapped her cane with her good hand. "About that. I've decided to return to the center with the rest of the elders. It's too remote living at the nursery, and I want to be with my friends."

"That's fantastic." Felicia looked excited to see her grandmother so content with her friend, but Declan knew she'd be sad to see her go, that she'd miss her.

"Mind? I expect them. As long as you bring your handsome boyfriend with you." Nana winked. Was she wearing mascara and lipstick?

Declan tucked Felicia into his side and planted a kiss to her head. "That is good news! I'm so happy for you, but you'll be missed."

"That's not the good news. I mean, that is good news, but not the good news we have for you," Davey stammered in a crush-on-Nana kind of way.

Declan decided to help the poor man out. "What's the good news, then?"

"You're innocent," Davey announced, as if Declan didn't already know that.

Felicia chuckled. "I'm glad you finally agree."

"You don't understand. Ms. Horton and Ms. Melba paid a visit to your mother, and she signed a document outlining what transpired and how it wasn't you but your father who had committed the crime." Nana rested her cane against the table and grabbed Declan's hand, squeezing it tight. "We're going to see to it that your conviction's overturned so you won't have to complete your probation, or make restitution, or worry about ever returning to jail again."

Declan wanted to believe her words, but he'd heard horror stories about long court proceedings, tons of money wasted, and never getting the results a person longed for. "I appreciate that, but I'm happy here. No need to spend that much time and money that we don't have to prove something we already know." He looked for confirmation from Felicia, and she gave a nod.

"There's an organization that helps with this stuff, and we've already called them. They're going to contact Felicia on Monday. It's free to you, so nothing to lose," Davey announced, as if he'd done all this and more to make up for how he'd treated Declan when he'd first arrived. "Trust me. I fight for the people of Sugar Maple."

His words were better than any medicine. They were life-affirming, welcoming words that encircled Declan with love and comfort. "Thank you. This means more than I can say."

Felicia took Declan's hand and squeezed. He could feel her happiness and excitement.

Declan shifted between feet. "Did my mother say anything else? Does she want to see me?"

Nana sighed. "I'm afraid not, son. Not because she doesn't love you. According to Ms. Horton, your mother can't face you because of failing you when your father committed the crime."

Felicia stood on her toes and kissed Declan's cheek. "We'll keep trying. She'll come around."

The crowd flooded toward the gazebo, catching all their attention. "Is it that time already?" Declan checked his watch. "We better get over there now. I don't want any of us to miss this."

"What's going on?" Felicia asked.

"Your friends are getting a surprise. One you don't want to miss." Declan took her by the hand and led her to where there was an opening in front of the gazebo, where Stella and Carissa sat on the bench. Drew and Knox both lowered to one knee in front of their girlfriends.

Felicia squealed along with Mary-Beth, and Jackie tried to hide it, but Declan saw her smile.

Cheers and hoots sounded from all around.

"How perfect. The entire town's here to share in their happiness," Declan whispered into Felicia's ear.

"You knew about this?"

"Knew? I helped plan it."

Drew held out a ring, and Carissa's squeals must've reached the nursery. Stella looked more like she was hit by a truck, but when Knox handed her the custom ring made out of metal from the scrap parts of the Chevy bumper, she shifted from road kill to a hundred and twenty on a back road, throwing herself into his arms so swiftly he fell back with a thud.

Felicia clapped along with everyone else. "I don't know. I'm not sure about this proposal."

"Really? Why? You like Drew and Knox, right?" Declan asked.

"Yes, of course. It's not that." She smiled up at him. "I just think I'd prefer a quiet proposal for just two people, intimate and romantic."

Declan thought he'd jump out of his skin with excitement. He knew it was too soon, but that didn't stop him from imagining what was inevitable once they settled back into life. "I'll keep that in mind. When do you think is the best time of year for a proposal?"

"Fall. This is Sugar Maple. Everything's perfect in the fall."

"Then I look forward to fall in Sugar Maple more than I look forward to my next breath, because I love you, Felicia Hughes, and I want to spend the rest of my life with you."

The End

ABOUT THE AUTHOR

Ciara Knight is a USA TODAY Bestselling Author, who writes clean and wholesome romance novels set in either modern day small towns or wild historic old west. Born with a huge imagination that usually got her into trouble, Ciara is happy she's found a way to use her powers for good. She loves spending time with her characters and hopes you do, too.

ALSO BY CIARA KNIGHT

For a complete list of my books, please visit my website at www. ciaraknight.com. A great way to keep up to date on all releases, sales and prizes subscribe to my Newsletter. I'm extremely sociable, so feel free to chat with me on Facebook, Twitter, or Goodreads.

For your convenience please see my complete title list below, in reading order:

CONTEMPORARY ROMANCE

Winter in Sweetwater County

Spring in Sweetwater County

Summer in Sweetwater County

Fall in Sweetwater County

Christmas in Sweetwater County

Valentines in Sweet-water County

Fourth of July in Sweetwater County

Thanksgiving in Sweetwater County

Grace in Sweetwater County

Faith in Sweetwater County

Love in Sweetwater County

Sugar Maple Series

If You Keep Me

(Coming soon)

(A prequel Christmas Novel)

If You Love Me

If You Adore Me

If You Cherish Me

If You Hold Me

(Coming October 2020)

If You Kiss Me

(Coming December 2020)

Riverbend

In All My Wishes

In All My Years

In All My Dreams

In All My Life

A Christmas Spark

A Miracle Mountain Christmas

HISTORICAL WESTERNS:

McKinnie Mail Order Brides Series

Love on the Prairie

(USA Today Bestselling Novel)

Love in the Rockies

Love on the Plains

Love on the Ranch

His Holiday Promise

(A Love on the Ranch Novella)

Love on the Sound

Love on the Border

Love at the Coast

A Prospectors Novel

Fools Rush

Bride of America

Adelaide: Bride of Maryland

YOUNG ADULT:

Battle for Souls Series

Rise From Darkness

Fall From Grace

Ascension of Evil

The Neumarian Chronicles

Weighted

Escapement

Pendulum

Balance

Made in the USA
Las Vegas, NV
16 September 2022